Monique had dreamed of kissing Mac this way, with all the hunger her healthy woman's body had stored for so long. She stood on tiptoe, her arms reaching around his neck, stretching her body like a lithe cat, burrowing closer to him, her tongue intertwined with his in the most sensuous of slow dances. She answered his moans with little sounds of her own, wanting it to go on forever. . . .

Good heavens, what was she doing? This wasn't a romantic dream, it was the real thing; and she was being entirely too easy. What would he think? She backed away from him.

He looked at her through heavy-lidded eyes. "I almost forgot Jerome's waiting in the truck. I'm glad one of us has good sense."

Yeah, one of us. She felt too embarrassed to look him in the eye. "Good night, Mac."

She discreetly stood at the window and watched him leave. His step had a jaunty spring to it. The window was closed, but she imagined him whistling a happy tune. And why not? By kissing him with such uncontrolled ardor, she'd practically told him she was willing to be his bed partner while he was here in town.

It would be a difficult impression to erase.

BOOK YOUR PLACE ON OUR WEBSITE AND MAKE THE ARABESQUE ROMANCE CONNECTION!

We've created a customized website just for our very special Arabesque readers, where you can get the inside scoop on everything that's going on with Arabesque romance novels.

When you come online, you'll have the exciting opportunity to:

- View covers of upcoming books

- Learn about our future publishing schedule (listed by publication month and author)

- Find out when your favorite authors will be visiting a city near you

- Search for and order backlist books

- Check out author bios and background information

- Send e-mail to your favorite authors

- Join us in weekly chats with authors, readers and other guests

- Get writing guidelines

- AND MUCH MORE!

Visit our website at
http://www.arabesquebooks.com

BETTYE GRIFFIN

Straight to the HEART

ARABESQUE
BET BOOKS

BET Publications, LLC
http://www.bet.com
http://www.arabesquebooks.com

ARABESQUE BOOKS are published by

BET Publications, LLC
c/o BET Books
One BET Plaza
1900 W Place NE
Washington, DC 20018-1211

All Kensington Titles, Imprints, and Distributed Lines are available at special quantity discounts for bulk purchases for sales promotions, premiums, fund-raising, and educational or institutional use. For details, write or phone the office of the Kensington special sales manager: Kensington Publishing Corp., 850 Third Avenue, New York, NY 10022, attn: Special Sales Department, Phone: 1-800-221-2647.

First Printing: January 2004
10 9 8 7 6 5 4 3 2 1

Printed in the United States of America

for Gary A. Griffin

ACKNOWLEDGMENTS

While it's true I wrote this book and all my books all by my lonesome, I wouldn't have done as well without the encouragement, support, and just plain enthusiasm of the following folks:

Family First: My husband Bernard Underwood, my mother Eva M. Griffin, my sister Beverly Griffin Love, my brother Gary A. Griffin. My aunt Juanita Morton, and uncle Chester E. Morris. My niece Alisha Griffin Baez, and the East Coast grand-nieces and nephew: André Dickerson (AKA "Shorty Red,") Melody Stokes-Baez (my leading salesperson!), Chavay Dickerson, Nydia Baez, and Serenity Baez.

The homegirls from Yonkers, NY: Phyllis Kalafus Antenucci, Janice Jones Blackwell, Cheryl McFadden Charles, Carolyn Harmon-Crute, Dorothy Hicks, Wanda London, Lois Mazziotta, Rebecca West Ogiste, my cousin Charlotte Ryer, Denise Turner, Sheila Tyler, and my cousin Lillian Morton Walton.

The home fellas: Jim Britt, my cousins Raymond Morton and Robert Morton.

The Golden Girls: Mrs. Gertrude "Trudy" Baynard, Mrs. Madeline "Peggy" Black, Mrs. Dorothy "Dot" Gill, Mrs. Josephine "Jo" Johnson, and Ms. Esther Sanchez.

Not quite a Golden Girl: Mrs. Barbara Bagley.

Former coworkers Judith Brome, Helen McCoy,

Marge McGill, Maxine Smith-Pendarvis, Inez Robinson, and Joan Starost.

Longtime friends Sharon McDaniel Hollis, Rhonda McDaniel Tirfagnehu, Christina Whitely, and Donald Whiteley.

The homegirls from Washington, NC, also known as the Lonely Hearts Club: Barbara Smaw Guilford, Retha Banks Williams, Velma Jones Dorsey, the late Dianne "DeeDee" Gibbs Griffin, and the Lonely Hearts Wannabe who used to run after them, Brenda "Peaches" Gibbs Gorham.

Relatives of relatives: Joyce Love Bethel, Rosemarie Mitchell, and Barbara Qualls.

Laura Gonzalez of Comcast in Jacksonville, Florida.

Ann Abrokimas and Lillian Tyee of New Little Branches Day Care in Yonkers, New York.

Kendra Lobos of the Washington, NC, Chamber of Commerce.

The book clubs: PRIDE (Felice Franklin), Prominent Women of Color, Avid Readers & Reviewers of Jacksonville (Jackie McKinney), the Camden County Page Turners (Lisa Spindle), and RAWSISTAZ (Ann Brown).

And a very special thank you to Elaine English, Marcia King-Gamble, Dawn Henderson Stewart, and Kimberly Rowe-Van Allen.

Chapter 1

No More Man

There was no sunshine in Stone Mountain, Georgia, the day after the breakup.

Monique welcomed the sight of heavy fog outside her window that December morning. It wasn't a dangerous fog, like the type that made it impossible to see more than ten feet in front of you and caused pileups on the highway. This fog was just enough to shroud the surrounding area with a creepy white pallor, giving a forlorn appearance that matched her mood. Once again, she'd lost at love, and when she lost the last thing she wanted to see was a blue sky and brilliant sun. She wanted to open the window and shout, "Pluck!" Monique didn't swear—she felt it wasn't ladylike—but sometimes she needed a word stronger than usual to get her feelings across, so she'd adopted an acceptable substitute.

She seethed at the memory of last night. She and Gregory had been dating for nearly six months. The last thing she expected to hear from him was that he had reconciled with his old girlfriend. Actually, he said he'd merely *wanted* to reconcile with her, but Monique wasn't falling for that. He'd probably made good and sure they were back together before he sat her down for that Dear Monique speech. No wonder he had picked her up so early last night. The night was still young when he'd brought her home. He'd probably gone straight to the old flame to give her the good news that he was no longer involved.

At least he'd chosen an unfamiliar restaurant to break the news. She truly would have been incensed if he'd tarnished one of her favorite bistros with unpleasant memories. She only wished he could have been as considerate with his timing. He knew she was about to have a birthday, and not just any birthday, but her fortieth. Christmas fell just nine days after that milestone, and of course New Year's Eve soon afterward. But while she was considering all these holidays and special occasions, she couldn't help remembering that he hadn't been acting right since Thanksgiving. That must have been when he had hooked up with the former girlfriend. And she was alone, again.

How had this happened? She never dreamed she'd be almost forty years old and still single. And if that wasn't bad enough, she'd been involved with some of the best catches around, and she'd lost them all. Men like Austin Hughes, the managing partner of one of the nation's leading hospitality consulting firms. She had been madly in love with him and was sure she'd get to be Mrs. Hughes when they dated back in New York six or seven years ago, but he ended up falling in love with one of the travel consultants on his payroll. They'd gotten married and settled in Colorado, where the company had moved its home base. The last she heard they had one child and were expecting a second.

She *had* managed to get engaged to TV newsman Skye Audsley, but she didn't get a happily-ever-after ending there either. It had looked like she might have until the day Skye shared with her the difficulties he was experiencing in looking for a live-in caretaker for his elderly grandmother. She resented the attention he was giving to the matter—it took away from the time he devoted to *her*—and made the rather callous suggestion that he place her in a nursing home. Furious, Skye broke off their engagement on the spot. Her friends in New York told her he had not only found someone to be his grandmother's caretaker, but he ended up *marrying* the woman he hired, of all people. When Monique heard about it she scoffed, saying it would never last, that someone of Skye's stature couldn't possibly make a successful marriage with household help, but according to their mutual friends, Skye and his wife were happy, living the good life in Westchester County with their twins, a boy and a girl. The last she heard Skye's grandmother was still alive. She had to be well into her nineties by now . . . and she still lived with them.

There had been other men, all successful, all handsome, but the end result was always the same. Sometimes they just didn't click, the chemistry simply wasn't there, which happened to everyone at one time or another. But nothing lasting had ever come of any of her relationships. It hurt to admit it, but every man she found desirable eventually broke it off with her. She knew she had to do some serious soul searching. There was clearly something wrong here, and all the evidence pointed to her. Something about her personality somehow turned off the men she dated. Could she have unwittingly exhibited behavior to Gregory similar to the thoughtlessness she'd demonstrated to Skye?

Well, things were going to have to change. Monique had always known there were more eligible women than men in the dating pool, but she never once considered she would be one of the ones left out of the mix. Monique Oliver simply didn't get left out of things. Besides, that wasn't the root of the problem. It wasn't like she had a particularly hard time getting dates, she just couldn't *keep* them.

Time was passing faster than ever. It was probably already too late to have that little girl she always dreamed of, but if she didn't do some honest analysis about the part she played in the end of her relationships, the only thing she could be certain of was that she would spend the rest of her life alone and wondering what the pluck happened.

"I'm sorry to hear about you and Gregory," Monique's friend Doreen said as she buttered a biscuit, "but I think what bothers you the most was that he was the one who broke it off. I mean, it's not like you were in love with him or anything."

"Doreen!"

"Come on, Monique, be honest. If you were in love with him, you would have known it by now, and you certainly would have told me about it. Not that you'd have to, because it would show on your face. You'd light up whenever you say his name. We've all been there."

"Well, I don't know. . . ."

"I think it was just a comfortable, convenient relationship for you, knowing you had an escort when you needed one, and getting some good sex out of it as well. Sort of an *in*-significant other."

Monique fidgeted in her seat. They were enjoying the breakfast bar at Shoney's, and those wood-back chairs with thinly cushioned vinyl seats weren't the most comfortable. "Doreen, I invited you to brunch so you could offer me some sympathy, not so you could tell me how I never cared about Gregory."

"I don't mean to sound critical, Monique, but I don't understand why you don't want to admit that you weren't in love with him. There's nothing wrong with dating someone whose company you enjoy, but like I said, six months is plenty of time to know if there's something there you can build on or if you're just going to have a little fun together until it peters out."

Monique sighed. "Well, he didn't have to wait until a week before my birthday. He knows how apprehensive I am about turning forty."

"Monique, I'm sure Gregory didn't set up to deliberately hurt you. We just don't get to control when things happen to us. It really wouldn't have been fair to you if he had celebrated your birthday knowing his heart wasn't in it. You probably would have noticed something was off, and when you learned the truth you would've been furious."

Monique leaned back in her seat and glared at her friend, who continued to eat calmly. "Remind me never to invite you anywhere if I'm looking to be comforted. Especially if it involves food." She was so distressed that she didn't even feel like touching the plate of scrambled eggs, home-fried potatoes, grits, and bacon she'd collected at the buffet, but Doreen's appetite was unscathed.

Doreen shoved a fork holding eggs covered in cheese and mushroom sauce into her mouth and washed it down with a slug of orange juice. "Again, Monique, I'm not trying to be unsympathetic. I just wish I could get you to understand that this really doesn't have anything to do with you. He never stopped caring for this woman, and if things work out for them this time around, I think it's wonderful. There's nothing more sweet than love recaptured. In the meantime, you really haven't lost anything. I know you, Monique Oliver. You're thinking your life will be over if you don't have a date for New Year's."

Monique pushed the plate away. This breakfast thing had been a bad idea. The very scent of it was making her ill, and Doreen wasn't helping. She'd always been a sucker for romantic fantasies, with all her talk of recaptured love and happy endings.

Then she remembered what else Doreen had said, a new reason to be distressed. "Oh, my. New Year's. I can't remember the last time I didn't have a date to see the new year in."

Doreen shrugged. "Donald and Jackie are giving their usual New Year's shindig. You can always arrive after midnight if you think you'll feel self-conscious about not having anyone to kiss at the stroke of twelve."

"Oh, shoot," Monique said, suddenly tired of it all. She pulled a pack of Salems out of her purse, put one in her mouth, and lit it. "I'll probably just extend my vacation in North Carolina until January second. It'll be nice to spend more time with my family, and I don't think I'll have a problem getting the time off. Things are going pretty well at work."

Chapter 2
No More Job

Monique smoothed her skirt and unnecessarily adjusted the lapel of her blazer. The director of the department had asked to see her. Perhaps she'd be able to kick off the new year with a promotion. There'd been all kinds of rumors going on since the Christmas party, when her supervisor had displayed wildly inappropriate behavior, like shimmying on the floor flat on her back and sitting on the lap of a male colleague, her legs crossed and her dress riding up high on her thighs.

"Hello, Jack," Monique said confidently as she entered his office. The framed crayon drawings by his children made a cheery but odd contrast to the somber dark wood desk and credenza.

"Monique, come on in. Close the door behind you, will you?"

She complied, then sat gracefully in one of the twin chairs facing his desk. "What's up?"

"Unfortunately, not our profits."

She didn't know how to respond. That was certainly an odd comment for him to make. She was a paralegal, not part of the accounting department.

"We've got to do some streamlining, Monique. It's not like we're closing the entire department, but things are bad enough where fifteen people have to go."

She drew in her breath. Surely he wasn't telling her *she* was one of the unfortunate fifteen . . .

"I'm sorry, Monique. You've been a wonderful worker . . ."

Oh, no, he was! A drum began to pound inside her head. "You're *firing* me?"

"You aren't being fired; it's a layoff. They're two different things. We fire people when we're not satisfied with their performance. We lay off people because we're in financial straits."

"But Christmas is next week, Jack!" It seemed like a rational observation, but the holiday was actually her last concern. Just two days ago she'd turned forty. In anticipation of the event, she'd bought a sports car last summer, a zippy Nissan 350Z. How was she supposed to pay for it with no job? How was she supposed to pay her other living expenses?

"It's also the end of the year. We've had to make some adjustments to next year's budget. Your salary will be continued for the next eight weeks, and then you'll receive your accrued vacation pay." He clasped his hands on his desk tighter than what appeared to be comfortable, the skin beneath his fingers whitening unnaturally. "I'm sorry, Monique," he repeated.

She shrugged, not wanting Jack to know how crushed she felt. "Well, I guess that's that."

"We're also prepared to offer our services to assist you in your job search. Resumes, references . . . Human Resources will be able to tell you more."

Monique forced herself to think clearly. "I can take care of my own resume, but some references would be nice." She glanced at her watch. Five minutes to five. No way could she hide in Jack's office until everyone left. He'd practically dismissed her, and she had the feeling he'd be putting on his coat and leaving as soon as she was out of his office. *Hmph.* He was probably anxious to stop off at the mall and get something pretty for his wife at Victoria's Secret . . . plus something naughty from Frederick's of Hollywood for Carol in the word processing pool, whom rumor had it he was sleeping with.

She accepted his good wishes, thanked him, and prepared to face her coworkers. If fifteen people in the company were being laid off, as Jack had said, chances were the word had already spread. Rumors in this office traveled faster than a 747.

The first thing she noted was that those who worked in cubicles were standing up under the pretense of talking to their neighbors, yet all eyes turned to her when she emerged from Jack's office. The word was out, all right. Under the circumstances she probably would have been just as interested to see the ex-employee's reaction at having been let go, but as the ex-employee she found it plucking insensitive. She faced them and announced flatly, "Yes, I've just been laid off."

Judy, one of the secretaries, came to stand behind her and patted her arm. "This is terrible!" she said. "I heard they've let several people go because of cutbacks so they can save some money. And just before the holidays, too."

Monique was determined to sound nonchalant, knowing her reaction and that of the other unfortunate workers would be the talk of the office on Monday morning. "Well, I guess these things happen," she said lightly. "But I'll be fine. I was going away for the holidays anyway. Now I won't have to hurry back."

"Did they give you a fair package, at least?" Judy spoke in a low voice, which struck Monique as ironic, since she knew anything she said would be quoted for the entire office after her departure.

"It was certainly fair," she said. "I really haven't been here very long, less than two years."

"I think that's the criterion they're using to determine who goes."

"I can't argue with the fairness of that." Suddenly Monique felt an urge to get out of there as soon as possible. "You'll have to excuse me, Judy. I'm going to clean out my desk." She forced herself to keep smiling as her coworkers patted her on the back and wished her good luck and a merry Christmas . . . two expressions that generally didn't go together and sounded strange to her ears.

It didn't take her long to collect her belongings. She had no family photographs or other mementos on her desk, just more practical things like a bottle of clear nail polish to stop stocking runs, a spare pair of panty hose in case it was hopeless, an emery board, a change of underwear, sanitary supplies.

Fortunately, she kept all her personal belongings in a small canvas tote bag, which she merely scooped up by its handles. She had some pending cases and work in progress, but that wasn't her problem anymore. Let whoever took over her workload figure it out. She had other things to worry about. She was forty, romantically unattached, and now unemployed. The holidays were right around the corner, and life was setting her up for one heck of a case of the holiday blues.

In the old days they used to suggest going out and buying a new hat as a good way to shake off the blues. Well, she didn't wear hats, but maybe she'd ring in the new year with a new look. The idea was the same, to feel good when she looked in the mirror.

Maybe a new hairstyle . . .

Chapter 3

No More Hair

Monique tapped her fingertips on the arms of the chair as she leaned back in the rinse chair. She'd shown Starla, her hairdresser, just the color of tawny reddish blond she wanted. She was determined to have a new look to go along with the new, improved Monique.

While she'd always liked the color, she'd resisted coloring her hair any lighter than auburn, feeling her complexion was too brown for anything lighter. But Starla reminded her that Tina Turner was about her complexion, "and she's worn her hair light for years and looks great." Monique had to agree. Now she couldn't wait to see the results.

"Stop being so nervous," Starla said. "I told you, you're going to look fabulous."

"If I don't, can I sue you?" Monique said with a laugh.

Starla laughed too, but then she made a gasping sound Monique found alarming. "Starla, what's wrong?"

"I don't understand . . . this never happened before."

"What is it?" Monique repeated. She pressed her elbows into the padded arms of the shampoo chair and tried to sit up, but Starla held her down. "Let me get the rest of this stuff out of your hair quick."

"I want to know what's wrong, Starla."

"We've got a problem. It's never happened before . . . I guess your hair just doesn't like the bleach."

"Did it break off?" She'd worn her hair as long as it would grow—about level with her shoulder blades—as long as she could remember. Was Starla telling her it was all gone?

Finally Starla wrapped a towel around her head. Monique sat up, the chair back automatically straightening to the upright position. She pushed the towel back, and what she saw brought tears to her eyes. What had been long, luxurious tresses an hour ago were now ragged, uneven strands, none of which were longer than half an inch. "Look at me, I'm practically bald!" she wailed. "Starla, how did this happen?"

"It must have been the bleach."

"But I thought dyeing was perfectly safe, as long as it's not done at the same time as a relaxer. It's been two weeks since you touched up my hair."

"Usually it's safe, but not one hundred percent."

"Well, now's a fine time to tell me that. I've got no hair left!"

"I could give you a real nice short cut, Monique."

"At a minimum," she said coldly. The terrified look on Starla's face told her she'd made her point. The lighthearted words about suing from just a few minutes before suddenly had a whole new meaning.

Monique stared at the remnants of her hair with a heavy heart. In the mirror's reflection she saw the sympathetic expressions of other clients. It was all she could do not to cry. Why were all these terrible things happening to her?

Chapter 4

Home for the Holidays

Monique removed her hat, prepared for her mother's horrified reaction. She wasn't disappointed. Julia Oliver was a woman of definite opinions, none of which she was shy about expressing.

"Good heavens, Monique, what happened to your hair?"

"Oh, a little mishap with hair dye."

"A little mishap? You're practically bald!"

"Thanks a lot, Mom." But Monique really couldn't blame her mother. She'd used those exact words when she first saw herself that awful day at the salon. But now she'd had time to become accustomed to the short natural cut Starla had given her.

"Well, look at you. All that beautiful hair gone. You didn't try to bleach it yourself, did you?"

"Of course not, Mom. I don't know anything about bleach. I've been going to the same place ever since I've lived in Atlanta."

"Well, no more, I hope."

"Of course I'll go back. We made a deal. I'll be getting free hair care for a long time. I think she was afraid I was going to sue her. She knows I'm—that I *was*—a paralegal."

"But was it really necessary for you to cut your hair that short?"

"Mom, there were two patches where the hair broke off completely. I really had no choice but to even it all out." She didn't want her mother to know that people who bumped into her from behind often said, "Excuse me, sir," only to cover their mouths in embarrassment when she whirled around with a distressed expression on her feminine face. Even the tellers at the drive-through expressed reluctance to give her receipts for her deposits, making comments like, "Is Monique with you, sir?" Monique now took special pains to prevent that mistake from happening, like not leaving the house unless she wore lipstick, large drop or hoop earrings, and ladylike shoes. She'd start wearing Reeboks again once her hair grew out a few inches.

"But it'll take years to grow your hair back again."

Monique smiled patiently. Her mother came from an era where women depended on their looks to ensure their position in life. The prettier the girl, the better her chances of landing a successful husband. Hair cut shorter than most men's, so much that scalp showed through if it wasn't brushed carefully, simply didn't fit into the equation.

"Well, the color looks very nice," her father said.

"Thanks, Pop." Leave it to him to find something positive to say. Frank Oliver was as easygoing as Julia was outspoken. Monique attributed their successful marriage to their opposing personalities, which somehow balanced each other. "Where's Uncle Teddy?"

"He's next door at the hotel taking care of something. He'll be back shortly," her mother said. "But Peggy's anxious to see you."

Monique instantly took off toward her aunt's bedroom. The compact one-bedroom home had originally been a carriage house on the grounds of the large Victorian house. After the renovation her cousin Reggie had used it as his bachelor pad until he took a job in Charlotte, where he met his wife. At that time Teddy and Peggy stayed on the first floor of the bed-and-breakfast, which they'd purchased after retiring. When Peggy's cancer returned they moved to the guest house so she would have more privacy.

Monique was pleased to find her aunt fully dressed and sitting in a reclining chair opposite the television. The bulk of Peggy's lavender sweat suit helped conceal her drastic weight loss. Chemotherapy had caused all but a few strands of her hair to fall out, revealing a perfectly shaped head; and her illness was also evident from the toll it had taken on her once-beautiful face.

"Well, look at you," Peggy said in surprise after Monique bent to kiss her. She ran a bony hand over her head. "Trying to copy me, I see."

"Oh, Aunt Peggy, you're so funny."

"I'll bet Julia had a fit when she saw you."

"Got that right."

"I know my sister." Peggy patted Monique's hand. "It's so good to see you. This is going to be the best Christmas of my life, with all my family around me."

Monique blinked back tears. It would probably also be Peggy's last Christmas. She'd deteriorated in the few months since Monique's last visit. Her eyes looked sunken, and the loose skin of her cheeks hung.

Peggy sat up. "Help me up, will you, dear? Now that I've seen you I'm going to lie down for a little while. Reggie and Gina will be here with the baby this afternoon, and I want to be rested up."

* * *

"Is Peggy all right?" Julia asked anxiously when Monique returned to the living room.

"She's fine. She's lying down so she'll have some energy when Reggie gets here." Monique sniffled. "Mom, she seems so weak."

"I know, honey. But that's why we're here, to enjoy our time with her."

Monique knew she'd start sobbing if she stayed there another minute. She had to do something, go somewhere, to calm down. "I think I'll go next door and see what Uncle Teddy's up to. Be back in a few."

She forged a diagonal path to the large Victorian house with a sign out front identifying it as Dodson's Bed-and-Breakfast. Painted lilac with a trim the color of butterscotch, the house looked like it belonged in a Sherwin Williams paint commercial.

The knob of the front door turned easily under her grip. Tinkling ceiling chimes announced her arrival. Her uncle sat at a desk in the parlor. Beaming, he rose when he saw her. "I told everybody my daughter was coming," he said jovially, holding out his arms. He and Peggy, the parents of one son, often referred to Monique as their daughter. Monique had spent most of her childhood and teen summers in Washington with them and Reggie. Her parents felt the country setting was a healthy change from the Bronx, where she was raised and where her parents still lived. "Hey, you cut off all your hair," he said after they embraced. "You aren't ill, are you?"

With all that was going on with Peggy, Monique felt it perfectly natural for that to be his first thought. "No, I'm fine," she assured him. "My hair broke off when I lightened it."

He took a moment to study her hair. "A suicide blonde, huh?"

"What's a suicide blonde?"

"That's an old expression for girls who dyed, D-Y-E-D, by their own hand."

"That doesn't apply to me, Uncle Teddy. First of all, my hair is more red than blond. Second, I didn't do this myself. My hairdresser botched it."

"I stand corrected. Have you seen Peggy?"

"Yes. She's getting some rest now. She was waiting for me to get in. Now she's looking forward to seeing Reggie and Gina and the baby."

"How was the drive?"

"Long. I'm glad it's over."

"I'm sorry I wasn't there to greet you, but I had to check in some guests."

"I didn't think anyone would be here over Christmas."

"Oh, sure. Lots of people have more company for the holidays than they can comfortably accommodate. Two of the four rooms are occupied. Your parents are staying in another, and I've got the downstairs room for you, because I have a booking for two days after Christmas. Reggie is staying with his in-laws. Good thing, too. Our policy is for no children under ten, and I can't overlook that when there're other guests here, even for my own grandson. It wouldn't be fair."

"Wow. Business is good. You've got your hands full."

"I wanted to talk to you about that, Monique. Sit down."

She sat, looking at him expectantly.

"Your mother tells me you were downsized."

"Yes. It came as a terrible shock."

"What are your plans?"

"To get another job, since my unemployment will

cover my car note, but not my rent. And, of course, I've got to eat and pay the light bill and other living expenses. I've already turned off my home phone. I use my cell for everything now."

"Any luck so far?"

"Not really, but this is just about the worst time of year to look for work."

He cleared his throat. "Monique, would you consider coming to work for me?"

"Doing what?"

"Running the B-and-B. I'm so busy taking care of Peggy. I bring her to the doctor in Greenville nearly every day to get a shot. It's getting more and more difficult for me to run things here, since I can't be in two places at once, and Peggy comes first. Reggie's doing well with that software design company in Charlotte. I can't expect him to give up his career aspirations to be an innkeeper. Besides, this isn't really full-time work. That's why Peggy and I didn't buy this place until after we retired."

"I don't know anything about being a host myself, Uncle Teddy. Most of my experience is in being a guest." While Monique was dating Austin Hughes she occasionally got to travel with him as he rated the quality of service given by his many clients. One time they'd even gone on a cruise.

"Oh, it's easy. Processing deposits, checking people in and out, and doing the grocery shopping for breakfast. All the guests are told to call with an estimated arrival time, because I don't want to hang around all day waiting for them. And you can handle the redecoration. I know how much all you gals enjoy buying furniture. The old place is starting to look outdated."

She was almost speechless. "It almost sounds too easy."

"It is. Most of the time will be your own. Even if you're on call in the evenings, you'll rarely hear from anyone. Lyman Watkins keeps the place pretty well maintained. It's just hard for me to be here to check people in and out. Connie, the girl I hired last year, does most of the work. She makes up the rooms for new guests—we don't provide daily cleaning, like hotels do—and she makes breakfast. She's been a real godsend since Peggy's cancer . . . after it came back." He cast his eyes downward for a moment. "I can't pay you much, but you'll have free room and board, plus cable TV."

"How much is 'not much'?"

He named a monthly figure, and Monique's mind swiftly went to work. He was right, it wasn't much, but the sum was fair, considering how little she'd have to do. It would cover her car payment plus her Nordstrom bill and the health insurance policy she'd purchased at a reasonable cost, since she'd enjoyed good health all her life. She was the type of client insurance companies loved— the kind where they could look forward to collecting her premiums each month with a low likelihood of her submitting in any claims other than for routine checkups. When all her monthly bills were paid she'd have sufficient, if not plentiful, pocket money. As long as she didn't have to dip into her savings she'd be fine.

"Can I think about it?" she asked.

"Sure. Something else to think about . . . you'll get to spend time with your aunt Peggy."

Monique always thought it odd that both he and Peggy pronounced "aunt" as a homonym for the insect. She'd looked it up once in the dictionary and learned that was actually the correct pronunciation, but regardless, she and most of the people she knew said "ahnt." She supposed it was just a cultural habit.

"She doesn't have much time left," he continued. "And you're one of her favorite people, after Reggie and me."

"Mom mentioned he's been driving in from Charlotte most weekends."

"He's a good boy, and he loves his mama. This is hard on him." Teddy's voice suddenly took on an urgent tone. "Monique, can you promise me you'll at least think about it?"

It was sounding better and better, but she couldn't make such an important decision so quickly. "I can do better than that, Uncle Teddy. I'll have an answer for you in a few days."

Chapter 5

No More Men

It didn't take Monique long to make up her mind. Her initial trepidation about Teddy's offer stemmed from the town of Washington itself. She'd enjoyed her youthful summers here, but as an adult the town of ten thousand seemed awfully dull. So what if it was the first incorporated town to be named after George Washington, way back in 1776, and was rich in history? Their mall didn't even have a decent bookstore. Everything was in Greenville, a fifteen-minute drive.

The visitors to her uncle's house helped change her mind. Liz Barkley, a distant cousin—their mothers were first cousins—stopped by and was thrilled to see her. Divorced with a sixteen-year-old daughter, Liz had returned to Washington when her marriage to an army officer ended a decade earlier. She was indignant when she learned Monique had been to town over the summer to visit Peggy and hadn't called, mollified only when Monique insisted it had been a quick weekend trip with no time to look up old friends. Liz gave her the lowdown on other people she had known, a surprising number of whom still lived in Washington or in nearby Greenville. Monique began to feel hopeful. Maybe life here wouldn't be so dull after all.

Monique's fears of being isolated were slightly eased

by the presence of Connie James. The housekeeper at
the bed-and-breakfast was a few years older than she,
forty-six, but had been tragically widowed when her husband succumbed to a heart attack while golfing over a
year ago. Monique felt it would be nice to have some
company, someone to shoot the breeze with over morning coffee. She had worked in an office setting for her
entire career, nearly twenty years, and didn't think she
could handle too much solitude. Sure, she'd be able to
keep Peggy company, as Teddy had suggested, but she
suspected that just a little of that would go a long way.
Peggy tired easily, and Monique certainly didn't want her
aunt to feel like she had to entertain when she felt weak
and was growing more so by the day.

One other thing provided the push Monique needed
to make up her mind for certain. A change of scenery
would go perfectly with her desire to regroup and work
on her personality, identify her shortcomings, and hopefully conquer them. Shucks, maybe she'd carry it one
step further to include bad habits and stop smoking.
That had been on her mind ever since Peggy began to
fail. Peggy's cancer wasn't tobacco-related, but Monique
couldn't help noticing how short of breath she became
while she worked out. She felt sure there was a connection between her gasping for air during exertion and
over twenty years of smoking a pack a day. If she kept it
up she'd likely need an oxygen tank in another twenty
years. Besides, cigarettes were expensive, and now her
funds were limited.

She couldn't say she wouldn't miss metro Atlanta,
Doreen, and the other friends she'd made, but in the
meantime there would be no more commuting in the
city's notorious traffic, no hard-on-the-wallet spending
sprees on sale days at Nordstrom's . . . and no more men.

Yes, no more men. She meant it. She was going to take full advantage of her time in this sleepy little town. While she was here she'd not only figure out why her relationships always tanked, but learn how to avoid that in the future, even if she had to reconstruct her personality brick by brick, like a house. The next time she got involved it would either have a happy ending or *she* would be the one to break it off, but she'd been dumped for the last time.

No more being dropped like a slippery watermelon.

Chapter 6

No More Men?

Monique wrapped up her business in Stone Mountain fairly quickly. Her landlord, who had a new tenant waiting, let her out of her lease when she provided written proof of her new job offer, and she arranged to have her furniture put in storage. She packed a few clothing items to carry with her and shipped the rest to Washington for storage in the basement of the bed-and-breakfast.

When she reached her destination in the afternoon she stopped at a convenience store to fill her tank. She discovered too late that the debit card payment option didn't work at the pump. Sighing in annoyance, she replaced the gas cap and went inside, hoping there wouldn't be a long line.

A middle-aged man clad in jeans and work boots approached the register, holding a plastic bottle of Icehouse and a bag of pork rinds. He wore a Carolina Panthers baseball cap, which he tipped in her direction. "Afternoon, ma'am," he said admiringly.

"Good afternoon," she said pleasantly, surprised at the attention. She had removed her sunglasses and wore a thick knit cap on her head to protect against the January cold, which she felt more than ever now that she had so little hair. Her hair was as short now as it had been a month ago. She'd gone back to Starla before she left and had the new growth cut off, removing all traces of the reddish blond dye job that caused her so much grief. Now she could concentrate on letting it grow out. Monique chuckled at the memory of Starla's face when she told her about her plans to leave town. Starla hadn't quite been able to conceal her delight at learning that Monique wouldn't demand normally expensive hair care for free as compensation for the loss of her hair.

"I haven't seen you around before," the man said.

"That's because I don't live here. I'm just visiting."

He smiled at her once more and then paid for his items, tipping his cap once more on his way out.

Monique moved into the spot he vacated directly opposite the cashier. The man at the register, handsome and dark-haired with gray temples, who appeared to be of Middle Eastern lineage, raised an eyebrow in approval and greeted her with a hearty, slightly accented "Hel-lo."

"Hi. Twelve dollars on pump three," she said, handing him her card. "Did you know that the debit card pay-at-the-pump option doesn't work? The whole point of having it is so customers won't have to come in the store and wait in line."

"It goes down every now and again. I'm sorry you were inconvenienced, but I'm glad you came in. You make this humble establishment that much prettier," he said graciously, then pointed to the keypad. "Enter your PIN, please."

She poked the four digits. What was with these guys, anyway? She hadn't remembered anyone in town being so flirtatious when she was here before. Even the way the clerk said, "Thank you, and please come again" when the transaction was complete was loaded with suggestiveness.

She shook her head as she went outside and got back behind the wheel of her Nissan for the short drive to the bed-and-breakfast.

The first thing she noticed was the sign out front, which now had two lights poised beneath it to illuminate it after dark. She began to feel excited about the prospect of redecorating the inn. She envisioned ceiling fans in every room, big easy chairs with ottomans, French Provincial TV tables with gracefully curving legs, and accent tables covered with the same fabric as the pillow shams and bed quilts.

She went to the guest house and greeted Teddy and Peggy. She quickly became alarmed by Peggy's rapid deterioration. Monique had only been in Stone Mountain for a few weeks, but in that brief time Peggy had lost more weight and now looked almost skeletal. With a choking feeling in her throat, Monique realized her aunt only had weeks left.

Monique's family was smaller than most people's. Her father was an only child, and Peggy was her mother's only sibling. Peggy and Teddy were the only aunt and uncle she had, and Reggie her only first cousin. Unlike many friends her age who had lost at least one parent, she'd never been through the bereavement of anyone close to her, and as the end of Peggy's life approached, Monique was becoming more acutely aware of how difficult the loss would be.

Both Teddy and Peggy were thrilled to see her. Peggy, too weak to shower, now received services of a home hospice, who gave her a sponge bath daily. She read a little, watched some of the old movies she loved on Turner Classics, but most of the time she just slept.

* * *

Monique quickly settled into a daily routine. After breakfast she worked with Lyman Watkins of Watkins Home Improvements, who held the maintenance contract on the inn, on the improvements she wanted to make. She frequently went out in the afternoons, often to Greenville to look at furniture and fabric, but forwarded the inn's calls to her cell phone to avoid missing a call and a potential booking. Other times she simply sat with Peggy while Teddy went out. He didn't like to leave her alone because of her weakened state.

Monique spent a few minutes doing accounting whenever she checked someone in or out. Teddy's manual bookkeeping system was simple and easily to follow, but she bought software and installed it on her laptop computer to automate it. She was no math whiz, and this way she didn't have to worry about making any errors.

She also fell into the habit of spending time with Connie after the guests had eaten, chatting over breakfast. Teddy provided all of his guests with a full breakfast as an alternative to the lighter continental breads and pastries the bed-and-breakfast also featured. Connie made spectacular melt-in-your-mouth pancakes, so tasty they all but guaranteed guest referrals and repeat bookings.

"These are wonderful, Connie," Monique exclaimed the first time she tasted them. "So light and fluffy. And a hint of a flavor I can't quite identify."

"It's a trade secret, just like in that movie *Imitation of Life*, the original version from the thirties. Except I'm not telling, like Louise Beavers did in the movie." She giggled. "You should see my son wolf these down when he's home on school breaks."

"I'll bet. These are restaurant quality, much better than even IHOP. I'm honored that you're here instead of working for our competition."

"Actually, I did some work for a caterer after my husband died, but I gave it up. The hours were too irregular for me." Connie looked a little embarrassed. "I'm afraid I'm a creature of habit. I like a routine. Occasionally I do some cooking and baking for them, though."

Monique looked at Connie curiously. About fifty pounds overweight with a sleek short haircut, she was quite attractive and made a good appearance, with her manicured active-length nails and discreet gold jewelry on her ears and circling her neck and wrists. She drove a late-model Chrysler convertible. Monique had the impression that Connie didn't work out of economic necessity, but of course that wasn't the type of question one could ask outright.

"Working here is perfect for me," Connie continued. "Just a few hours to make breakfast, clean the kitchen, vacuum, and it's a steady schedule. Of course, it takes a little longer when I have to get a room ready. Some of my friends thought I was nuts to take a job involving housecleaning, but I've always enjoyed anything domestic. I stayed home for about five years after I had my son, Glenn, but I went back to work part-time when he started school. I found a job at the school board, which meant I was off whenever school was closed. Eventually they laid me off to save money—"

"I know all about that," Monique said with a smile.

"Yes, I suppose you do. But I enjoy housework, and now that it's just me there's not much to be done at home. I like talking with the guests, too." She looked a little sad, as if she was thinking there was no one at home to talk to, either.

Monique rushed to keep the conversation going so Connie wouldn't have a chance to grow morose. "I noticed that most of the guests mentioned your name in the keepsake books we have in the guest rooms. You're very well thought of, Connie. Definitely one of our most valuable assets."

"Thanks. That means a lot to me. Working here helps fill the void in my life since Charles passed." She sipped her coffee, then quickly put the mug down when the chimes went off. "I'd better go see who that is."

"It's probably Lyman. He'll be coming by every morning to work for a few hours until the redecoration is complete." Seated in the dining room, she didn't see Connie pause in front of the oval mirror in the foyer to pat her hair and rub her lips together to distribute her lipstick evenly after eating breakfast.

Monique heard them talking before they entered the dining room. "Morning, Lyman," she called out.

"Mornin', sweetness," Lyman greeted as he entered the dining room. He squeezed her shoulder affectionately before sitting down at the table. "You're lookin' mighty pretty today."

"Why, thank you." She stifled a giggle. She didn't know what it was about the men in this town. It she didn't know better she would swear someone had sprinkled flirtation dust on all of them. Literally every man she saw offered sweet talk. Lyman Watkins was a burly fellow of about fifty, average looking but with a genial manner that branded him immediately likable, and even white teeth worthy of a Pepsodent commercial. She caught Connie's eye and smiled at her, but to her surprise Connie looked rather stony-faced, almost like she was mad about something.

"How 'bout some pancakes, Lyman?" Connie offered pleasantly, suddenly back to her old self.

"I'd love some, if you're sure it's all right." He glanced at Monique.

"Just think of it as a fringe benefit," she said with a smile. "We're going to be seeing a lot of you while you're working on the rooms."

"Thanks, Monique. I'm going to put the second coat on today. I'll have the ceiling fan in tomorrow."

"Wonderful."

"Are you doing one room at a time?" Connie asked, standing in the doorway to the adjacent kitchen, right across from the stove where four pancakes were browning in a large cast-iron skillet.

Monique started to answer, but closed her mouth when she realized Connie had directed her question to Lyman. She uncomfortably became conscious that Connie hadn't said anything to her since Lyman arrived. What happened to the carefree air of just moments before of two girlfriends chewing the fat at the dining room table?

"Yes. Monique thought it'd be easier that way," Lyman said in answer to Connie's question. "We have to plan around both your need for rooms and my schedule. But I'll be back later to move the furniture back after the paint dries, just in case someone needs the room tonight."

"I doubt we'll need it. Only one guest room is in use today, so we have two others available, but I guess you never know," Monique said.

"Most of the drop-ins are in the spring, summer, and fall, when the weather is nicer," Connie said loudly from the kitchen, where she'd gone to flip the pancakes.

"People dock their boats at the marina and come to check out the town or to play some golf."

"And you should see some of those boats," Lyman said. "Big enough to cruise to Bermuda in. They make up a good portion of Teddy's business. Let's face it. When you can afford a boat that big you don't stay at the Days Inn."

"I remember when Uncle Teddy used to take us down there when we were kids," Monique said dreamily. She was maybe ten or twelve. She, Reggie, Liz, and one or two other kids from the block used to pile into the back of Uncle Teddy's pickup truck and go see fireworks every Fourth of July over the Pamlico River. The Pamlico flowed straight into the Atlantic Ocean, and they used to admire the luxurious boats of the wealthy. She'd been so happy then, so carefree. No worries about her career, her looks, getting old, death claiming people she loved . . .

She abruptly cleared her throat and straightened her spine. This was no time for her to get carried away with emotion, especially in front of Connie and Lyman, although they both would probably understand. At least Lyman probably would. Connie was behaving so strangely. "Yes, I remember," she repeated, her voice strong. "So . . . today's schedule is all set?"

"All set, sweetness," Lyman said.

"If you'll excuse me, then," she said as she pushed back from the table, noticing but not acknowledging the hard set to Connie's mouth.

After breakfast Monique set up her laptop in the parlor. She knew she needed an outlet besides gardening, physical workouts, and billing. It had nothing to do with the lack of male companionship. Her creative side was crying out for satisfaction, and she'd decided to try to appease her urge by writing a novel. She'd always loved to read, but she couldn't always find something that appealed to her. That was when the idea hit to try and write something herself.

Monique had never lacked for self-confidence. She always felt capable of doing whatever she put her mind to, unless it involved education or training she didn't possess. Her attitude was that if other women wrote books, why couldn't she? But in spite of her strong faith in her ability, she kept her literary aspirations to herself. This way if she failed, no one would have to know about it. Years before, she had heard someone declare, "If at first you don't succeed, destroy all evidence that you tried," and adopted it as her personal motto. Success was to be celebrated. Failure was best kept hidden.

She picked up the phone on the console table when it started to ring. The caller identified herself as a representative of a construction company in Raleigh. "We'll need a reservation for one of our employees for one or two weeks, possibly longer," she said.

A two-week-long booking caressed Monique's ears like the prettiest of melodies. She went into an enthusiastic delivery of why Dodson's was the best choice among the bed-and-breakfasts in Washington, and the woman made a tentative reservation.

Monique noted all the information of the booking. The guest's name was Russell McDonald.

She read the reservation back to the secretary for accuracy and thanked her for her patronage. "We look forward to seeing Mr. McDonald next Sunday." When she hung up she wondered what type of situation would warrant staying at a bed-and-breakfast for two weeks. She doubted anyone had ever been a guest for that long. Mr. McDonald must not have a wife.

Not that it mattered to her. Men might be looking twice and coming on to her, but nothing could make her change her mind. No way would she date again before she was emotionally ready.

Chapter 7
He's So Fine

Monique removed the clean dishes from the dishwasher and returned them to the cabinets. The inn was empty, as the only guests had checked out after breakfast. She liked it when there weren't many guests on Saturdays and Sundays. Vacated rooms could wait for Connie to take care of when she returned to work Monday morning, but there was no postponing breakfast. She'd never been much of a cook. Thank heaven Teddy had a waffle iron.

She suddenly broke into a fit of giggles. How incredible for her to be running a bed-and-breakfast, of all things, the same business her old boyfriend Austin Hughes was in. He'd probably be proud of her.

Her smile slowly diminished as she continued to think of Ozzie, as he was known to his friends. Of all the men she'd dated, he was the only one she'd truly loved. She'd been heartbroken when he stopped seeing her, saying he had never been in love with her any more than she'd been in love with him, but he'd been wrong. Her feelings for him ran much deeper than mere contentment at having an escort when convenient, like the way she'd felt about Gregory. She had wanted to be Ozzie's wife, and the breakup devastated her.

Her feelings for Skye Audsley never truly developed

into love, although when they were dating she tried to convince herself she did and that he was the one she wanted to spend the rest of her life with. He was extremely handsome, with a trim mustache and a clipped baritone voice so perfect for TV, and she'd gone after him mostly because he and Ozzie had a social connection, a friend in common, Zack Warner. She knew Zack would tell Ozzie she was seeing Skye, and secretly she hoped that when Ozzie learned this he would try to get her back.

Skye might not have been the owner of a highly successful business, but his success nonetheless transcended that of Ozzie's. Skye's presence on national television made him instantly recognizable to millions of people. With his good looks, money, and fame, no wonder she repeatedly told herself she could learn to love him.

And Skye, eager to find Ms. Right and settle down, had responded to the interest she showed in everything connected to him and given her anything she asked for . . . until that day when she said the unforgivable. No wonder she hadn't connected to Skye's beloved grandmother. If she loved him the way a woman should love her future husband, she never would have viewed the old lady as a threat to be disposed of. Afterward she'd felt so ashamed of her behavior that she left New York and moved to metro Atlanta, but her efforts to reinvent herself there hadn't been successful, because she'd still been too stubborn to admit a problem existed.

She smiled again. Maybe she failed in Atlanta, but here in Washington, the home of her maternal ancestors, she wouldn't. She'd already figured out an important key to the flaws in her personality, and while neither insecurity nor insincerity was a desirable virtue, awareness could help her avoid such behavior in the future.

* * *

When her work in the kitchen was done she did some yard work. Her parents had always kept a small garden in the backyard of their Bronx home, and while she hated having to help out as a child she now found she enjoyed working with soil. Even the mundane parts, like pulling out seemingly endless weeds, were strangely soothing. But now her body tended toward stiffness and soreness when she'd been sitting for long periods. A hot shower would probably help. Then she'd visit with Aunt Peggy. She didn't want to stray too far from the inn today. Mr. McDonald, the seven- or fourteen-day reservation, was scheduled to check in this afternoon.

Monique showered in her private bath and dressed in jeans and a red crew neck sweater. She chose a pair of large red hoop earrings, just one of a large selection of costume jewelry she'd picked up in Greenville. She brushed her hair into place, then checked to make sure no scalp spots were showing. Her mother was sure to be horrified, but Monique had decided against letting her hair grow out. She found she rather liked the convenience of a short natural. She had joined a fitness center to help keep in shape, and liked the convenience of being able to wash her hair after a vigorous workout on the treadmill or a swim without the pain and discomfort of rollers and pins sticking into her head. One of her goals was to simplify her life, and it didn't get any easier than an every-two-week visit to a local barber.

The only downside to her new look was the noticeable sprinkling of gray that had sprouted seemingly from nowhere. She wondered if it was a reaction to the trauma of the dye, and she found it alarming. Now that she was forty, she had grown sensitive about aging. But at least her gray didn't seem to stop the men at the fitness center, plus others she came in contact with, from hitting on her. She didn't understand why she suddenly attracted men the way toy departments attracted children, but she'd be lying if she said she didn't enjoy it.

She slipped on a red wool blazer to guard against the late March chill, then went out the back door and crossed the backyard to the guest house.

Teddy wasn't there, but Peggy wasn't alone. Her cousin Sarah Henderson—Liz's mother—was with her.

"Hello, Aunt Sarah," Monique said while simultaneously squeezing Peggy's hand. Sarah was actually her second cousin, but since she was the same age as her mother and Peggy, Monique used the prefix "aunt" out of respect.

"I'm so glad to hear that you're staying on in Washington for a while, Monique. We're all thrilled to have you here. Peggy tells me you're redecorating the inn," Sarah said.

"Yes, I am," she said, taking a seat next to Peggy on the couch. "Lyman Watkins does all the maintenance. He's already started painting. The first room's going to be a royal blue. Next he'll be wiring for ceiling fans."

"Royal blue is a lovely color, but you do realize a dark color will make the room seem smaller," Sarah remarked.

Monique suppressed a smile. Her mother had made the same comment. Funny how women of the same generation tended to think alike. "Yes, but the closet, window trim, and baseboards will be white, and I'm going to furnish it with a white wicker set from that import place in Greenville."

"That sounds lovely, Monique," Peggy said. "I knew you wouldn't let Teddy down. He's been so worried about how he was going to run the business and take care of me at the same time. You've always been such a good girl."

"Thanks, Aunt Peggy."

"I think it'll be good for Liz to have you around, too," Sarah added.

Monique could only manage an uncertain smile. She had no idea what Sarah meant. How could her being in Washington possibly benefit Liz?

Sarah bent and brushed her cheek against Peggy's. "I'll go now so you two can talk. Teddy'll be back from the store any minute. Tell him I'll see him tomorrow."

"All right, dear. Thanks."

Sarah put on her jacket and left.

Peggy turned to Monique. "Teddy went to run an errand, since Sarah was here with me. Between her and Bitsy down the street—she just lost her husband, you know, to a heart attack—someone comes over just about every day so Teddy can get out of the house for a few minutes, but they never stay more than an hour or so. I think they're afraid of tiring me out."

"At least they're considerate. It's good to see you sitting up today."

"I actually feel pretty good."

"I'm glad. Aunt Peggy, what did Aunt Sarah mean when she said my being here will be good for Liz? Anyone would think we were impressionable children, not forty-year-old women."

"Oh, Liz's had a bit of a rough time. She's been divorced for years, you know."

"I knew that. I remember when she moved back here with her daughter."

"Well, ever since then she's been looking for a new

husband. I'm afraid that over the years she's gotten somewhat of a reputation as a man-chaser."

"Oh."

"After all, Washington's a small town, and people do talk."

Monique stared at a patch of carpet. She could just imagine what the people who knew her had had to say when Skye Audsley broke off their engagement. Peggy had told her how excited everyone was when she was going with a nationwide news broadcaster, but she was too polite to mention any reaction to the news it was over, and at Skye's pronouncement.

Peggy patted her hand. "I think she'll benefit from being with you, too, even if I didn't say so in front of Sarah. You two have always been close. Maybe you can help her find her way. She needs to, for her daughter's sake. It's not good for children when their mother's reputation has a blemish on it."

Monique stayed at Peggy's for nearly two hours. Teddy returned and made them lunch. Peggy, feeling tired and having only picked at her food, then went to lie down.

"I hope you're not regretting your decision to stay in Washington," Teddy said as he helped Monique clear the small round table.

"Not at all. I'm enjoying myself."

"You aren't bored?"

"Oh, no. There's plenty to do. I'm busy picking out quilts and curtains and throw rugs for the rooms, and of course deciding what colors to paint each room. I've got ideas for a new design to plant flowers, and . . ." She trailed off, then decided she could trust him with what she hadn't confided to a single soul. "I'm even trying my hand at writing a novel."

"You are!"

"Well, we can keep that one between you and me. I don't know if anything will come of it, but in the meantime I'm having fun. I love to read, and many times as I'm reading I find myself saying, 'I could've written that.' Now that I have some free time, I want to see if I've really got it or if I just *think* I've got it."

"I'm sure it'll get published. You can do anything you put your mind to, Monique."

"Oh, there's my cell phone." She flung the dish towel across her shoulder and rushed to her purse, pulling the small phone from an outside pocket. "Dodson's Bed-and-Breakfast. Oh, yes, Mr. McDonald. Yes, that's right. Sure. I'll be here. Just call if you have any trouble finding us. All right. Good-bye." She hit the *end* button. "That was our soon-to-be guest. He said he'll be here in about two hours. He's driving from Raleigh."

"Is that the fellow who's staying two weeks?"

"Yes. It's a business-related stay. A secretary made the reservations. A construction company. She mentioned it might even be longer than two weeks, but she wasn't sure."

"Nothing like a nice, long booking. Good for the pocketbook."

"This is the first time I spoke to him directly," Monique said thoughtfully. "I didn't know—well, he sounds black." Actually, he had a great voice, deep and sexy, the kind of voice that should belong to a marvelous-looking man. But she knew a great voice didn't guarantee great looks. She'd been fooled before at work. Male visitors of any race whom she thought would be movie-star handsome based on their voices usually turned out to be three hundred pounds or had bad skin or yellow-tinged teeth, or other unappealing physical traits.

But of course it didn't make a bit of difference to her what Russell McDonald looked like. He could have Denzel Washington's smile, Morgan Freeman's voice, and Samuel L. Jackson's tall, slim physique. All she wanted from him was his money. Or his employer's money, since they were the ones footing the tab for the extended stay. Her mind was made up. She could admire men from a distance, but there would be no involvement with anyone until she had her act together.

"Just make him comfortable so the other people from his company will want to stay with us when they come to town," Teddy said.

Monique silently agreed.

She was working on her manuscript, typing directly into her laptop while seated at the desk in the parlor. The large house was quiet and still, other than the soothing sounds of a Kenny Rankin CD that always spurred her creativity. The doorbell caught her off guard. She laughed, feeling foolish, after her upper body jerked at the startling sound. Of course, it had to be Russell McDonald, her standing reservation.

She unlocked the front door and made sure she wore a big smile before opening it. But the pretense of pleasantry soon became genuine with one look at the gorgeous man on the other side of the door. "Hello. Mr. McDonald?"

"Yes," he said in that melodious voice she remembered from the phone. "You must be Ms. Oliver."

"I am. Welcome to Washington, and to Dodson's Bed-and-Breakfast. I hope you had a nice drive."

"I did, thanks. Found it with no difficulty. The directions you provided were excellent."

"Glad to hear it." She opened the door wider and stepped back to allow him to enter as the chimes tinkled a welcome. "Follow me, please, and I'll get you checked in."

The moment her back was turned Monique put her lips together as if she were about to whistle, which of course she didn't do. How nice to have a good-looking man like Russell McDonald sleeping under her roof. Her body literally tingled at the thought that they were the only two people in the house, even if his room was upstairs.

He was a tall man, about six one, but as far as she could tell from his unzipped brown leather bomber jacket, he was in good physical condition. No belly protruded. Gray hairs streaked his mustache and short, neat beard. His head was covered by a baseball cap, but she'd been so taken with him she didn't notice what team.

"Is this your first time visiting Washington?" she asked.

"Yes, it is. I'm from Raleigh. But I wouldn't say I'm here on a visit. I'm a construction foreman. My employer is putting up a subdivision of seventy homes here in town, and the original foreman had a heart attack and then decided to retire. That put them way behind schedule, so they brought me in to take over."

"Oh, I see."

"I'll be in town for an extended time, about a year, but unfortunately I won't be spending it all as your guest. This is a lovely establishment"—he briefly looked around the comfortably furnished parlor—"but the company's already looking for a furnished apartment for me. It's more economical for them."

"I understand." Her mind raced for something she could say, preferably something that would yield some information about his marital status. She might not be ready to date now, but if Russell McDonald was going to be in town long enough to build a subdivision he'd probably still be around when she *was* ready . . . and he looked better than anyone else she'd seen in Washington. She might as well learn now if there was any point in thinking about it.

When she finally hit upon something appropriate, she said, "I think you'll find our town a very friendly place, but I guess it'll be difficult for you to have to travel back and forth to Raleigh to see your family."

"Oh, it's not that far, just about a hundred miles. I can be home in less than two hours."

She smiled to mask her disappointment. She didn't care how many hours it took him to drive home. What she wanted to know was if he had a wife. He wore no wedding band, but a lot of married men didn't, and not necessarily because they stepped out on their wives. In his case, construction work might be hard on jewelry.

"The paperwork is all made out," she said. "I've multiplied the nightly rate times seven and added tax."

"I've got a corporate credit card right here." He pulled his wallet out of his hip pocket and unfolded it, handing her a Visa that bore the name of his employer.

She gave him the rules of the house while the card processed. "Checkout time next Sunday is by eleven A.M. Breakfast is served every morning in the dining room, which is right through there." She gestured with her hand without pointing. "You can come down for breakfast any time between seven and nine A.M. on weekdays, eight and ten on Saturday and Sunday.

"Your room is equipped with cable television, DVD player, telephone, minirefrigerator, and a second line for Internet access," she added, continuing with her standard speech to new guests. "Your private bath has cleaning supplies in a wicker basket in the corner. Since your reservation is for two weeks, you'll be interested to know that we provide complimentary room and bath cleaning and fresh linens every seven days. If you'd like service more frequently, there's a ten-dollar charge."

"Would I be able to get an extra face cloth and towel before that?"

"You'll find two sets in your room now."

He nodded. "In that case once a week will be fine."

She nodded. "Uh . . ." Goodness, she was going blank. What was wrong with her? She'd given this speech dozens of times since she'd been here.

But not to anyone who looked as good as Russell McDonald.

"Where was I?" she mused, stalling for time to collect her thoughts. She told herself it wasn't Russell McDonald's tall, dark, and handsome appearance that had her flustered, but rather the spiel about the housekeeping service, since they rarely had anyone who stayed more than three or four nights.

But all the self-assurances in the world wouldn't matter if she couldn't remember the rest of her little speech. The result would be the same. *He'll think I'm a plucking idiot.* She felt goose bumps forming on her arms as she struggled to recall the lines she'd recited so many times before. Her brain felt frozen, and she could hear the uncharacteristically loud ticking of her Timex watch, which suggested a countdown to a bomb detonation. Each passing second helped spur her memory, and she finally resumed speaking. "Local calls are free." She searched her memory wildly for the one thing she'd forgotten to tell him. "Oh, yes. Your private bath is equipped with a hair dryer." She stopped talking when she realized he was laughing. No one had ever found her amenity description amusing. "I don't get it. What did I say that was funny?"

He removed his cap to expose a shaven head. He ran his hand over the shiny skin and smiled brilliantly, as if he were modeling.

They laughed together, his baritone and her higher-pitched laughter bouncing off the walls, and suddenly the room felt a lot warmer.

Chapter 8

Home Away From Home

Mac opened the door to his room and placed his bags on the floor. He inspected it and was satisfied. The room with its cinnamon-brown walls and French Provincial furniture was pleasant, with more warmth than a standard hotel room. Yes, he'd probably be quite comfortable here for the next week or two.

He hadn't wanted to take this assignment, didn't like the idea of living away from home for so long, but the company was in a real bind, and refusing them wouldn't feel right. They'd done all right by him over the years. Besides, he was the only foreman who wasn't married, so there were no complications of being away from a wife and children.

But being unmarried didn't mean he had no familial responsibilities. As the oldest of seven, with both parents now dead, he played a prominent role in the lives of his younger siblings, particularly two of his sisters who were raising their children alone. Germaine's kids were still rather young, and she had an ex-husband nearby who helped out, but Donna was widowed and had special needs. She suffered from systemic lupus, which sometimes flared up with skin lesions, arthritic pain, and fevers. Her illness was difficult on her children, seventeen-year-old Jerome and fourteen-year-old Shaun. They lived in Mac's mother's house, and all three of them had been deeply affected by her death last September. With her passing, Donna had lost her major source of emotional assistance, and Mac tried to help fill it. Ever since his father died he had spent considerable time with Jerome, feeling the teen needed a man's influence in his life. He would have to get Jerome here for weekends now and then once the company found him an apartment. Shaun was old enough to see after her mother, and Mac's sister Cora, whose children were also teenagers, would assist.

Company would be welcome, since it didn't look like he'd have much to do. Washington didn't look like a town with a brisk social life. He wondered what Monique Oliver did to occupy her time, besides come on to men.

He instinctively knew she was single from the way her face lit up when she opened the door for him. She was certainly a pretty woman, and normally he'd be glad to meet her halfway and see what came of it—his love life had been pretty boring lately—but a sixth sense told him not to. Her demeanor seemed just a little too cute, a little too coy for him, like the way she'd fished to try to learn his marital status. It gave him the uncomfortable feeling that she was anxious to stake a claim on him if he was available. Then, after he had revealed his shaved head and given them both a good laugh, he'd thanked her and addressed her formally, and she promptly invited him to call her Monique in a tone that defined seduction. It was almost laughable. She might not have batted her eyelashes at him, but her comments and mannerisms weren't very subtle. She was about as genuine as cubic zirconia. He was so put off by the vibes she was putting out he almost forgot to tell her that everyone called him Mac. The expectant look on her face after she provided her own first name reminded him of the need to reciprocate.

Yeah, she was pretty—he found her natural haircut refreshing after seeing various women in his life, both sisters and lovers, continually fuss and despair over their tresses—but from what little he'd observed of her he felt she knew it. She struck him as the type who would want 100 percent of any man who showed interest in her.

Best to steer clear, he thought. Surely there were other equally attractive women here in Washington who didn't feel everything had to revolve around them.

He smelled the coffee brewing as he descended the stairs at seven-fifteen the next morning, his jacket over his arm. After he ate he'd head straight over to the construction site. No need to go back upstairs to get his jacket.

Six chairs and place mats were in place at the rectangular cherry-wood table in the formal but cozy dining room, its walls painted a warm tomato-red and the flavorful aroma of bacon in the air.

He was about to sit when he was caught off guard by a cheerful, heavyset woman who emerged from the adjacent kitchen. Where was Monique?

"Good morning, Mr. McDonald," the woman greeted. "I'm Connie. I make breakfast each morning, and I also handle housekeeping."

So Monique didn't do breakfast or housecleaning. He should have known. She hadn't seemed like the type. "Good morning, Connie. And please call me Mac." It made him uncomfortable to have Connie, who appeared to be about his own age or perhaps a little older, address him so formally. If she was a hotel maid it'd be different, but the atmosphere of a bed-and-breakfast was more personal. For all he knew she was a part owner.

"All right, Mac it is. How about some bacon and eggs to start your day? The bacon's already done. All I need to know is how you like your eggs."

"Good and scrambled," he said as he sat down and reached to pour himself some coffee.

"I know exactly what you mean. None of that runny stuff. I'll have them right out." She placed a small wicker basket on the table. "In the meantime, I've got some biscuits right out of the oven."

"Thanks." He pushed away the linen cloth covering the basket's contents and pulled out a golden-brown-textured biscuit. "I guess no one else has come down yet, huh?"

"You're actually our only guest. But someone else is due in tomorrow."

"How many rooms do you have here for guests?"

"Four."

"Do you frequently have only one room occupied?"

Connie shrugged. "This time of year, yes. This is our slow season. It'll pick up after Easter, and that's just a few weeks away." She turned at the sound of sizzling. "Excuse me. I think the pan's ready for your eggs."

The doorbell chimed, resonating through the first floor. A feminine voice called out, "I'll get it, Connie."

Moments later Monique appeared, closely followed by a burly jean-clad fellow. "Good morning," she said cheerfully.

Hellos went back and forth, and the man pulled out a chair and sat at the head of the table. "I'm Lyman Watkins," he said to Mac. "I'm making some improvements to the inn, so you'll be seeing me most mornings."

"Mac McDonald. Pardon me for not shaking—"

"It's all right. I see you're buttering your biscuit. I'm gonna fix one of those myself." Lyman reached for the basket.

Connie placed a plate of eggs, bacon, and home-fried potatoes in front of Mac.

"Thanks, Connie," he said. "By the way, these biscuits are fabulous."

"Glad you like them."

"Gonna fix me some eggs over easy, Connie?" Lyman asked, eyeing Mac's plate enviously.

"Monique's got it. She likes hers the same way, with an intact yolk. Then when she cuts it with a fork that raw yellow filling runs all over the place." Connie shuddered. "Give me firmly scrambled any time."

Mac laughed. He liked Connie's natural warmth. "I'm with you on that one."

"Here we go," Monique said, carrying two plates, setting one in front of Lyman.

"Thanks, sweetness."

Mac stole a quick glimpse at Monique and Lyman. Were they an item? After all, she'd run to answer the door when he rang, she'd personally fixed his breakfast although Connie just told him she handled the cooking, and he called her "sweetness." If Lyman was Monique's boyfriend, Mac had misunderstood her motives for trying to learn if he was single. Maybe she had a girlfriend she wanted to hook him up with. Not that he'd be interested. Any friend of Monique's was likely to be cut from the same self-centered cloth.

But Monique didn't seem to be paying special attention to Lyman. She took a seat opposite Mac and called over her shoulder, "Connie, why don't you fix your plate and sit down with us?" Then she looked up and smiled. "I see we're all getting an early start this morning," she said.

Mac shrugged. "I want to get to the construction site by eight."

"One of my clients has a clogged kitchen sink, and I told her I'd be over by eleven to run a snake through it," Lyman said, "and I can't get over there until I'm finished here. You do construction, Mac?"

They began discussing building. Mac stole a glimpse at Monique, who appeared bored by the technical conversation, as he expected her to. As the hostess, he felt, she should be gracious about whatever topic her guests chose to speak about. All right, so Lyman wasn't a guest, but he was. But Monique stared downward at her plate as she ate, her lower lip poked out slightly like a spoiled child's.

Connie came in from the kitchen, plate in hand. Mac was talking with Lyman, but he saw her quick frown and her gaze jump from Monique to Lyman before she moved to sit on Monique's other side. He wondered what it was all about. Was there some kind of romantic triangle going on?

"Well, that was just great," he said as he pushed his chair back and got up. "I'm starting the day with a full belly."

"It's a rule of Dodson's. No one ever leaves our table hungry," Monique said with pride.

"I'll probably be too full to eat lunch. Good-bye, all."

"That Mac is sexy-looking, isn't he?" Connie said as she wiped her mouth after finishing her breakfast. Lyman had gone upstairs to begin work, and only she and Monique remained.

"I suppose," Monique said with a shrug.

"Do you realize it's only a quarter to eight and breakfast is over? I don't think we've ever eaten so early. What brings you in at this hour?"

"I didn't sleep well last night." Monique wasn't being untruthful. Sure, she'd wanted to see Mac at breakfast and try to make a good impression, and she'd felt terribly let down when he had more to say to Lyman than her, but she'd tossed and turned throughout most of the night, her mind awash with uneasy thoughts. It bothered her that after just one look at Mac she was ready to chuck her promise not to pursue any men until she'd worked on herself thoroughly. Just because she'd made the promise to herself didn't mean it was any less important than a promise made to anyone else. Lyman's affectionate manner toward her was probably her penance for breaking her word. It was bound to give Mac the wrong idea.

But what Mack might think about her and Lyman was really secondary, because her biggest concern was Peggy's worsening condition. As happy as Monique had been to hear her aunt felt better, she couldn't deny how awful Peggy looked. She feared Peggy might be experiencing one last burst of strength before the end.

Chapter 9

Man About Town

"How's that, Monique?"

She accepted the hand mirror the barber offered her. She held it up and rotated slowly in her chair to get the full effect. "Good job, Tom," she said, handing the mirror back to him.

"I neatened out your hairline in the back, but I followed the natural line, the way you like."

She laughed. "It must be hard, keeping up with all your customers' personal preferences."

"Not really. It just comes natural after a while, and I've been doing this a long time." Tom took a brush and gently swatted at her hairline and neck, then unhooked the cape that covered her and shook the loose hair from it.

Monique reached in her purse for her lipstick. She always felt a little self-conscious after a haircut, and painted lips gave her feminine confidence. She never again wanted to be mistaken for a man.

There was little chance of that happening in her present company, however. "Monique, when you gonna go out with me?" old Pete Frazier said as he slowly ambled to take her place in Tom's barber chair.

"Now, Mr. Pete, I told you, I'm taking a sabbatical from dating. There are other things I'm concentrating on right now."

"Aw, you just haven't met the right man."

She lowered her eyes, pretending to be concentrating on counting out bills for Tom's payment and tip, which she'd done before she left home. *Yes, I have.*

She paid Tom, telling herself not to think about Mac. He'd been at the B&B four days now and barely looked at her. She'd never been so frustrated, and it didn't help that just about every other man she came in contact with wanted to get close to her.

"So how long you gonna be on this sabbatical?" another man asked. "I wanna know so I can take you out when it's over."

She couldn't believe J.T. was asking her out. While Pete was probably close to eighty, J.T. was still in his twenties. What was that old song her mother used to sing as she cleaned the house? "They're Either Too Young or Too Old."

"Oh, I don't know," she replied breezily.

"Whatchoo talkin' 'bout, J.T.?" Pete said, sounding like Gary Coleman on that old sitcom. "You can't be takin' Monique or nobody out when you work most nights."

"I can, too. I'm off Friday and Saturday nights, now that I have seniority at the call center."

"Y'all need to leave the poor girl alone," Tom said. "Can't you see she don't want to be bothered with either one of ya?"

Monique silently blessed the happily married barber. "Well, fellas, I need to be on my way. Thanks, and I'll see you again in two weeks."

She opened the door against a chorus of good-byes, stepped out, and practically collided with Mac, who was on his way in.

"Oh, excu— Well, hello, Mac. What a nice surprise to see you here."

"You too. I've missed you at breakfast the last few days."

Her heart did a little leap. Did he really mean it, or was he just trying to be nice? "I usually eat a little later, with Connie, after the guests have finished." She didn't think Mac, as the only guest, would object to her and Connie and Lyman joining him for breakfast. Since they were all contemporaries, she felt Mac might even enjoy the company. But now that there were other guests at the inn, she didn't feel it was proper for the staff to mix with paying customers. Lyman was an exception, for he was an outside contractor.

"Your hair looks nice. You just had it cut?"

"Yes. Tom's an excellent barber. He'll do a good job—" She stopped abruptly, not knowing how to complete the sentence. Mac was bald, so surely he wasn't here for a cut.

"I need to get my head shaved."

Oh, of course. Even men with shaved heads needed maintenance. If his head hadn't been covered by his trademark baseball cap she would have realized.

"One of the guys at work recommended him, and knowing you go to him makes me feel better. Your hair always looks sharp."

"Thank you, Mac," she said, pleasantly surprised at the compliment. "Sometimes I get a little self-conscious when I'm just out of the chair. People have been known to mistake me for a man."

His reply came swiftly. "Anyone who mistakes you for a man needs their head examined."

She laughed, certain he was only being polite. "I'll try to remember that the next time it happens. But I'm sure you'll be pleased with Tom's work." She suddenly became aware of J.T. watching them curiously from inside the shop window. Was there anything worse than a male busybody? "Well, I guess I'll see you later."

"See you." Mac smiled after her, then went inside and greeted Tom and his patrons. An elderly man was in the chair, and a younger man was sitting in a straight-back chair, skimming today's newspaper. At least Mac assumed it was today's paper. The oblong coffee table in front of the chairs held tattered magazines that had obviously been around awhile. Mac glanced at them. A *People Weekly* cover, obviously over two years old, featured the still-chilling sight of the Twin Towers of the World Trade Center ablaze. An even older *Jet* magazine showed Toni Braxton in costume for her role as Belle in the Broadway production of *Beauty and the Beast.*

He noticed Tom's curious glance and knew what the barber was thinking before he said the words.

"You must be new in town."

Mac chuckled. "Yes, I am. I was brought from Raleigh to work on the new subdivision they're building off of Fifteenth Street. My coworkers told me you're the best barber in town."

That met with cheers, and then the younger man startled Mac by asking, "You know Monique?"

He felt his features harden. His first thought was to say, *What's it to ya, Junior?* Instead he said, "I'm staying at Dodson's."

"Oh, Teddy's place," Tom said. "I cut his hair, too."

"Nice girl, that Monique," the elderly gent said. "I've been trying to get her to go out with me for weeks. I hope you have better luck than I have."

Mac tried to hide his amusement. This old guy asked

Monique out? He was two generations before her time. Maybe two and a half.

"Yeah," the young man Mac had christened Junior added, "but she says she's on a sabbatical and she's not goin' out with anybody."

He arched an eyebrow. Sabbatical from dating? That didn't sound like Monique. She seemed to thrive on male attention, and from what he'd seen she got plenty of it. Then again, she might have fibbed and merely said she was suspending all dating just to get these fellows to stop bugging her. Chances were they were around whenever she came in. The old guy—he was too old to still be working—probably didn't have anywhere else to go, and Junior, who looked like he needed a trim, didn't seem to be in a hurry to get it. When Tom finished Grandpa and gestured to Junior that it was his turn, the younger man told Mac to go ahead. Yeah, he probably liked to hang around the shop all day. Maybe he was unemployed and bored.

"Maybe you're the one who'll get Monique to change her mind," the septuagenarian said as he took a seat back in the waiting area.

The others all seemed to think that was funny. Mac chuckled himself, but for a different reason. Grandpa and Junior might be disappointed that Monique had refused them, and they obviously thought he felt the same way, but he knew better. She was cute, but he trusted the instinct that warned him to steer clear.

He saw Monique around the inn over the next few days, usually sitting at the parlor desk working intently on a laptop. He wondered what she was doing. Surely there couldn't be that much involved with running a bed-and-breakfast. But on Friday when he had to return to his room midmorning to retrieve a key he'd forgotten, he found her by the door chatting with the mailman, a fellow about his own age.

"Mac, you have mail," she said, holding out a nine-by-twelve goldenrod envelope sealed with colorful Priority Mail tape.

"Thanks. My sister must have spotted some bills in my box. She promised to forward them promptly." He took the envelope and uttered a standard "How ya doin'?" to the mailman, who nodded in return. Mac had only gone a few steps when he heard the mailman say to Monique, "So how about tonight?" He nearly tripped over his own feet as he temporarily stopped and strained to hear her reply, but quickly continued moving. He chided himself for being so nosy. What Monique did with her social life was none of his business.

He had a full weekend himself. Tonight he'd agreed to join the fellows for an after-work beer or two to celebrate the end of another grueling workweek. And technically it wasn't even the end—tomorrow they'd put in a half day to help get caught up from recent heavy rain. Tomorrow evening he'd been invited to a colleague's home for dinner. Sunday he had unofficial plans to join Lyman for the NBA game.

Like Monique said, the people of Washington had shown him kindness and consideration, and already he felt at home. He'd had breakfast with Lyman a few times at the bed-and-breakfast, talking sports, and their support of opposing pro basketball teams that happened to be playing this weekend led to an invitation to see his team, as Lyman put it, "get creamed."

Mac had a hunch that dinner at his colleague's would include a female dinner partner chosen by his colleague's wife. He disliked being set up, because his experiences had never been successful, but of course he would be pleasant to the woman while simultaneously being careful not to lead her on in the event he wasn't attracted to her. But who knew? Maybe this time would be the charm. He hadn't met any women in town yet, and if he had a female companion to spend time with maybe he wouldn't be so concerned about what Monique Oliver was doing.

When he walked into the neighborhood bar late Friday afternoon after work and saw Monique sitting in a booth with another woman, he knew she'd turned the mailman down. Knowing this somehow made him glad, but also puzzled him, because he didn't understand why. It wasn't like *he* was interested in any of the games she appeared to play. Why should it matter to him who her playmate was? Being good to look at was one thing, but why couldn't he get her out of his mind?

"Omigosh, it's him," Monique said, her words rushed and breathless in excitement.

Liz looked puzzled for a moment. "Oh, you mean your guest, the good-looking guy from Raleigh you were telling me about?" She started to turn around.

"Wait, Liz!" Monique hissed. "I'll tell you when." She waited a few seconds until Mac turned his head the opposite direction. "Okay, look now. He's at the bar, the one with the shaved head."

Liz wasted no time turning her head. "Oh, fine. Now that you tell me to look, I can't see his face, just his glow-in-the-dark head."

"He just had it shaved yesterday. He's turning now. Just be discreet."

"Mmm," Liz said when she turned back to face Monique. "No wonder you're so captivated. He's cute."

"I wish I knew how to get him to notice me. He's very polite, but it's all so impersonal."

"Go say hello to him."

"No, Liz. I'm not the aggressive type. This is a small place. He'll see me eventually. Let him come to me if he wants."

Unfortunately, when Mac did say hello, he only did so in passing. She would never know if he would have asked to join them, for Fletcher Hawkins, who had grown up with Liz and whom Monique knew from summer vacations of her youth, had slipped into the booth next to her uninvited and made no rush to leave.

Monique was appalled at Fletcher's lack of decorum. He and Liz had known each other all their lives, but only casually. Fletcher nonetheless voiced an enthusiastic "Hi!" when he saw Monique and slipped into the booth next to her, staring at her dreamily. She looked at Liz helplessly, but Liz merely shrugged.

Monique began to suspect that Fletcher was intoxicated. His eyes wore a glassy expression, and he smelled strongly of alcohol. When he spoke, his words came out garbled.

"It was so nice seeing you again, Fletcher," Monique said with what she hoped he would take as finality. "It's been a lot of years."

"Yuh lookin' good, Monie," he mumbled in reply. "Whus yuh phone number? I'll call yuh sometime."

This was ridiculous, she thought. Would he get up and leave already? "I'm sure we'll see each other around town every now and then, Fletcher. Maybe your calling wouldn't be such a good idea. You and I know we're just friends, but my boyfriend might think I'm cheating on him." She felt the lie would be excused because it was done to be polite. She couldn't come out and tell him that pluck no, she wasn't going to give him her phone number. If this didn't work, she'd merely excuse herself. He'd have to get up to let her out.

"Yeah, awright. I guess I be movin' on. See yuh, Liz." He planted a kiss on Monique's cheek so wet he might as well have spit on her, grabbed his highball glass, and lurched the few steps to the bar.

Liz shook her head. "Poor Fletcher. He's already known as a notorious drunk."

"I could kick myself for not sitting on the outside of the booth, but I never dreamed anyone would be so brazen," Monique said, frowning as she wiped his saliva from her cheek with a cocktail napkin.

"If I know Fletcher, he would have told you to just move over. The man doesn't have a nerve in his body."

"If he did, it's been saturated by alcohol," she muttered as she glanced about the room. "I don't see Mac. Oh, pluck, I think he's left." She could just smack Fletcher for monopolizing her that way. That could have been Mac sitting with her for twenty minutes. That's all it would take for her to make him see that she was witty and charming, that he was missing out by not talking to her more. If he were to ask her out she knew she'd say yes, promise or no promise.

"What is it with you these days?" Liz said. "I ask you to come out with me for a drink, and you get all the attention. Not that there's anybody here I haven't known for years, but that's not the point."

"Yeah, I get attention, all right. From everyone except the one I want to talk to." Monique slid to the edge of the booth, purse in hand and a half scowl on her face. "I need a cigarette." She'd done well with cutting back on her tobacco use, restricting it to mornings, after meals, and at bedtime, but pluck, this was an emergency.

Chapter 10
End of the Road

Teddy brought Peggy to the hospital the following Tuesday, after she complained of pain in her back and shoulders.

Monique rushed over to Greenville to join Teddy at the emergency room immediately after checking in a new arrival. "How is she?"

"They've got her pain controlled with morphine, so she's feeling better. They're getting a room ready for her. Monique, we're not full next week, are we?"

"We're full now, but as of right now we've got plenty of availability for next week. Why?"

"You'd better make sure to hold a room vacant for your parents in case they need to come down."

She caught her breath. "You think . . . ?"

"The doctor says he doesn't think Peggy'll be leaving here," he said quietly.

"Oh, Uncle Teddy!" She linked her arm through his, her fingers holding fast to his upper arm. She'd tried to steel herself for this, but she wasn't ready, she simply wasn't. But now she had to think of her uncle. "Did you want me to call Reggie?"

"I'll call him when I get home. I'm not going to stay long. Peggy's asleep. They tell me she'll be groggy unless she rallies, but they're not optimistic." He patted her arm with his free hand. The important thing is that we stay calm. We all knew it would come down to this."

That doesn't make it any easier. "I'll call my mother later, Uncle Teddy. That'll be one less thing you'll have to do."

Monique went to the hospital in Greenville every day. The male hospital staffers all smiled at her as she passed, and some voiced pleasant greetings. While she'd always welcomed male attention, so much of it was getting tiresome, to the point where her smile felt frozen on her face.

She spent about an hour with Peggy every morning, and although Peggy slept most of the time and didn't always know she was there, Monique nonetheless knew she was doing the right thing. *She* knew she was there, even if her aunt didn't. There wouldn't be many more opportunities to hold Peggy's hand.

Having a full house at the bed-and-breakfast helped ease the emotional strain. Four young women checked in to the two remaining available rooms on Wednesday, in town from their various cities of residence to be attendants at a friend's wedding, and they were obviously thrilled to be together again and were having a wonderful time, laughing and playing music in the parlor until eleven P.M.

And Mac was very much in residence. Monique couldn't understand why he failed to respond to her subtle hints. How ironic that the only man in Washington and Greenville who interested her didn't look at her twice. Maybe it was some type of sign, a reminder of the vow she'd broken by trying to get him to like her. Two months in Washington simply wasn't enough time for her to accomplish the deep, honest soul-searching she needed to do before going back out in the world of dating, and in her heart she knew it. But why should she let Mac slip out of her fingers and into some other woman's arms?

Monique couldn't deny that Peggy's decline had her feeling more stressed than usual. She tried to meet it head-on by working out furiously at the fitness center in Greenville. There were one or two such places right here in Washington, but she had joined the one her cousin Liz belonged to so they could work out together in the evenings, after dinner. She knew Liz preferred going to Greenville because she was constantly on the lookout for new men.

Now that Monique had lived in Washington for a few months, she understood precisely what Liz's mother meant by saying Monique would probably be a good influence on Liz. Monique had never seen anyone like her cousin. Liz never let a potential opportunity to flirt pass her by and played the "what if . . . ?" creative exercise to utter excess. If a man so much as held a door open for Liz, Monique believed she immediately began daydreaming of the possibility of him becoming her next husband. It had gotten old real fast, and Monique had to face the discomforting fact that she had more in common with Connie than she had with the cousin she'd known all her life. Connie was the one who accompanied her to Greenville on shopping trips to look for unusual furnishings for the bed-and-breakfast; Liz had declined so many times Monique didn't bother to ask her anymore.

Now that Peggy was hospitalized, Monique usually stopped by for a quick session in the morning after she left the hospital, since she was already in town. She hated to admit it, but she preferred working out alone, without Liz's sharp eyes scouting the male clientele and commenting on their physiques, which Monique found distracting.

She patted her tummy, which reflected the definite beginnings of a pouch. The way she'd been eating these days she truly needed a daily workout. Breakfast had become her favorite meal of the day; she awoke licking her lips in anticipation. Connie certainly was outdoing herself these days. After serving standard fare of bacon and eggs last Monday, in subsequent days she'd whipped up breakfast burritos, French toast, and cheese and mushroom omelets with her famous but calorie-laden biscuits on the side. The guests loved it, and Monique did, too.

She had to find pleasure in *something*.

Mac lowered the volume of the CD player. Was that grinding noise he heard coming from his truck?

He heard it again, and at the same time felt the steering wheel become stiff, then his alternator light came on. He quickly signaled that he was pulling over and with considerable effort steered the heavy vehicle onto the shoulder.

Damn. He had a cell phone and membership in an auto club, which made breakdowns a lot more bearable, but he wasn't even sure where he was, other than on Highway 264 somewhere between Washington and Greenville. He supposed the tow truck could find him.

He took his cell phone from the clip, then realized he needed to be able to tell them where to tow it. The tow truck driver would surely make a recommendation, but Mac was wary of disreputable connections and kickbacks. Better to call the site first. Surely one of the guys could recommend a good mechanic.

No one answered the phone in the trailer. Doggone it, was everybody out to lunch? He waited a few minutes and tried again with the same result. Well, he couldn't just hang around. He had things to do. Besides, it was cold out here. Maybe someone at the B&B could help him. He searched his wallet for the business card he had stuffed inside when he checked in.

The line was answered promptly. "Dodson's Bed and Breakfast. Good afternoon."

He was relieved at the sound of a feminine voice, knowing it was either Monique or Connie. He didn't care which. Either one of them should be able to tell him what he needed to know. "Hello. Mac McDonald here."

"Hi, Mac. It's Monique. Is everything all right?"

"Not really. My truck conked out on me somewhere on 264. I wanted to tell the tow truck where to take it in Washington. Can you recommend an honest mechanic?"

"Sure. Fields Auto Repair." She named the street it was on. "Mr. Fields has been in business for years, and they say he's as honest as the day is long. Were you on your way to Greenville or on your way back?"

"I'm going back. I had a meeting at the regional office this morning. Why do you ask?"

"Because I'm in Greenville myself. I can pick you up."

"You're in Greenville? I don't get it. Didn't I dial the hotel?"

"I forward calls to my cell phone when I'm out. Actually, Connie does it for me just before she leaves for the day, because I'm usually out."

"Oh. That's awfully nice of you, Monique, but I'll just

hitch a ride with the tow truck. I'm going to call the auto club now and have them get somebody out here."

"All right. I'll be here for another half hour or so, but I'll keep an eye out for you. You drive a green Explorer, right?"

"Right."

"Okay. If you're still there I'll stop by just to make sure you're all right.

"Oh, I'm sure it'll be fine. Fields, you said, right?"

"Yes. I'll let you go so you can call them. See you later."

Mac immediately dialed the auto club. The dispatcher said it would be thirty to forty minutes before help would arrive. He asked them to hurry before replacing his phone on his belt clip. He watched the cars zoom past, rubbing his arms and trying not to think about how cold it was.

Fortunately for him, the tow truck showed up just twenty-five minutes later. A grateful Mac got out to talk to the driver. He stood out of the way while the driver loaded the truck onto the flatbed, turning his head at the sound of a car braking on the shoulder. He recognized Monique's sporty burgundy Nissan.

His eyes remained on her as she emerged and walked toward him. She wore gym shoes and thick socks over bike pants that hinted at generously proportioned, shapely legs, and a camel-colored jacket that ended at her midthigh. A multicolored knit cap protected her head from the cold.

He moved to meet her, suddenly no longer interested in watching the tow truck driver secure his SUV to the flatbed. Although dressed casually, she looked luscious, a warm and welcome sight on a blustery February day. Her personality might leave him cold, but he found her face and figure appealing with a capital A.

"Everything okay?" she asked.

"Fine. It was nice of you to stop."

"I wouldn't feel right just driving past without making sure you were okay."

"Wow. Try getting that service from the manager of a Holiday Inn."

She laughed. "You're sure I can't offer you a ride back? I can drop you at the construction site."

He glanced at the tow truck and made a quick decision. "That might work out better, actually. The driver can bring the car to the shop, and you can bring me back to work. I can always get one of the guys to drive me to pick up the truck."

"Do you really think it'll be fixed before the end of the day? It's nearly noon already."

"Unless Fields is swamped with cars this afternoon, it shouldn't be a problem. I think it's just a belt that broke. Nothing major. They can have it running within forty minutes tops." He shrugged. "You're sure I'm not keeping you from anything?"

"Positive."

"All right." Mac glanced at the tow truck. "I think he's got it all loaded. I just need to sign the order, and I'll be right with you."

"I'll be in the car. It's cold out here."

The driver had the papers all made out, and Mac quickly signed, stuffing his copy into his jacket pocket. He thanked the driver and then quickly walked to Monique's car. He hoped he'd fit in the two-seater; it looked awfully small. She had the heat on, and the temperature inside felt comfortably warm. "Ah," he sighed as he settled inside, the heat instantly embracing his chilled body. But his knees were up against the dashboard. "You don't mind if I move the seat back, do you?"

"No, go ahead. I gave my cousin's daughter a ride the other day, and she's real petite, maybe five three. She moved it up."

He pushed back to a comfortable position. "Nice ride."

"Thanks. I always wanted a sports car. I decided if I didn't get one now I'll soon be too old."

"Too old? That's crazy."

"For men it's different. You can drive something like this twenty years from now and you'll look great, even if your hair is Reddi-Whip white. But if I get any more gray in my hair people will start to laugh at me. That's the way society thinks. It's okay for middle-aged men to try to look young, but when a woman does the same it's viewed as pitiful." Society definitely wasn't sympathetic to women's woes, not with gossip columns always sniping about the alleged plastic surgery various women stars had, but remaining quiet when brown-haired men in their fifties suddenly became blond and tight-faced in obvious efforts to look less paternal next to the generation-younger women they escorted, actions Monique interpreted as equally absurd. It wasn't fair.

She sighed. "If I've learned only one thing lately, it's not to put things off. Life's too short."

She looked grim as she gripped the steering wheel. He knew from Connie that Monique's aunt was ill. She was clearly having a hard time with it.

"How's your aunt?" he asked quietly.

"She's about the same. My parents are driving down on Sunday. They'll stay at the B-and-B."

"That reminds me, Monique. I'm going to be checking out Sunday myself. I just learned this morning that the company's found me a furnished apartment. I love staying at Dodson's, and I'm especially going to miss those great breakfasts Connie makes, but the company can't really afford to keep me there for the entire length of this assignment."

"We'll miss having you stay with us, Mac. I'm glad you were comfortable, and I hope you'll recommend us to your friends. Washington is a nice weekend getaway from Raleigh, and it'll be especially lovely in the coming months."

"I'll be sure to do that." To his embarrassment, his stomach grumbled loudly. He glanced at his watch. "Yes, I suppose it is about that time. Hey, why don't you let me take you to lunch? Even if you were in a hurry to get back to the B-and-B, you've still got to eat."

"Sure, I'd like that. I'm not in a hurry."

"You'll have to suggest a restaurant. I really don't know the area well yet." He was glad he had plenty of cash on him. Monique would probably select something expensive. Since he'd been in town he'd only noticed the usual low-budget fare, Burger King, the Golden Corral, Taco Bell, and his two personal favorites of that ilk, KFC and Subway. But surely there were one or two good restaurants overlooking the picturesque Pamlico River.

"Well, I'll tell you," she said. "I've got an urge for Bill's Hot Dogs."

He looked at her incredulously. "Bill's Hot Dogs?"

"Yes. They're the best hot dogs I've ever tasted, and I'm from New York, where they make some pretty good ones. Real comfort food." She paused a few seconds. "I could use some comfort right about now."

He didn't know what to say. Her voice cracked a little, like she was holding back a sob. He knew what was foremost on her mind. "You're very close to your aunt, aren't you?"

She didn't seem surprised that he knew the situation.

"Yes. She's been so brave through this whole ordeal. I never really thought she would lose the fight until I saw her last summer. That plucking cancer is eating her up."

He wondered if he'd misheard her, but he didn't want to ask her to repeat what sounded very much like a curse word. "I know what you mean," he said instead. "My father died of a stroke and went rather quickly, but my mother had stomach cancer. It was difficult to watch. Fortunately, she didn't suffer long. Just a few months after her diagnosis she was gone."

She took her eyes off the road long enough to look at him sheepishly. "I suddenly feel like a moaning idiot. As much as I love my aunt, I'm grateful to still have both my parents. How long has it been since you lost yours?"

"My dad passed away four years ago. I lost my mom just a few months ago."

"I'm so sorry, Mac."

"Thanks. Losing your parents is never easy, but it was especially hard for my nephew Jerome. He was real close to my parents. He and his sister and their mother still live in their house. Now that I've got an apartment here he'll be able to come down to spend weekends with me."

"It sounds like the two of you are tight."

"He's a teenager, and I've kind of been a father figure to him. My sister's husband died in an accident years ago."

She took the turnoff into Washington and headed for the hot dog stand that had been a local institution since the 1920s. Soon they were munching on franks and potato chips.

Monique closed her eyes as she savored the flavor of her hot dog dressed with mustard, relish, sauerkraut, and a dab of coleslaw, just the way she liked it. Funny how the old and familiar could have such a consoling effect on a person's psyche.

Mac bit into his chili dog. "Hey, these *are* good."

"I told you. The superrich have been known to send their private jets to pick up fifty or sixty at a time for their parties." She was pleased to have learned something personal about her handsome guest, especially now that he would be leaving the inn. She hoped he wouldn't be offended if she asked a question about his private life.

"You don't have children of your own, do you, Mac?"

"No. I've never been married."

"Neither have I."

"I never expected to be able to say that. Here I am, forty-three years old and still a bachelor."

"Neither did I. It's not so bad for a man. I turned forty a few months ago. I thought by now I'd be all settled down with a couple of kids. Now it'll probably never happen."

"Oh, you never know. It might not be too late," he said. "Actually, I already feel like I've been there and done that. I'm the oldest of seven, and all my brothers and sisters have kids. Being the bachelor means you're everyone's favorite baby-sitter."

"It must have been fun, being part of a large family. I'm an only child," she said wistfully.

"You don't know how many times I wished I was an only child when I was growing up." He chuckled. "Did I hear you say you're from New York?"

"The Bronx. My parents still live there, but Washington is my mom's hometown. A lot of her relatives still live here, cousins and things." Again she pictured Peggy lying in her hospital bed, and the magic was broken.

* * *

"I'm going to have to remember where this place is," Mac said when they were finished eating. "I definitely want to come back. I'm glad you brought me here."

"I'm surprised none of the fellows at work mentioned it."

"So am I. Most of them are from Greenville, but if people send private jets to pick up orders, I'm sure Bill's reputation extends at least to the next town." He wiped a few crumbs from his mouth with his napkin, then crumpled it.

"I'm glad you enjoyed it. Ready to get back to work?"

"Yes, if that's all right. I'll call the garage from there."

"Sure. Let's go."

Mac waved to her as she drove off. He could see the pain behind her smile. Her aunt's illness weighed heavily on her spirit. She was grieving from her heart, and she seemed very different, so much softer than his first impression of a woman made of plastic who was out only to capture the attention of every man she saw. He conceded that he might have judged her too hastily. From what he saw now there was a lot more to Monique Oliver than just fluff.

Chapter 11

Farewell

Monique sat in the front pew, along with her parents, Teddy, Reggie, and his wife. Peggy's closed casket was just a few feet in front of them. The strumming of a guitar soothed her pain, and she was glad Teddy accepted his neighbor's offer to provide the music. It might be unorthodox in a traditional community—she'd noticed some raised eyebrows and whispers among the congregation and knew they were speculating—but she found organ music depressing.

The service was over in less than forty minutes. They slowly filed out, and when Monique saw the sunshine she fought back an urge to run toward it with outstretched arms. At a time like this she had to restrain herself and be dignified.

She sighed with relief after climbing into the limousine next to her mother for the ride to the cemetery. The hardest part was over.

The grieving had officially begun when Teddy came to the inn Tuesday morning to tell them Peggy had died. A hospital staffer had called him shortly after midnight, saying Peggy's breathing had become labored and the end was near. He and Reggie made it to Greenville just in time to hold Peggy's hands as she quietly passed away. Teddy didn't feel it necessary to awaken them with the news and instead informed them first thing in the morning.

After a well-attended wake on Wednesday evening, they'd all said teary good-byes to Peggy at the funeral home this morning before the funeral. In accordance with Peggy's wishes not to be buried barefoot, Monique slipped pumps on her feet, and Reggie placed a teddy bear in the crook of her arm. Teddy then ordered the casket closed. Then they left for the brief graveside service. Because none of them could bear to watch Peggy's casket lowered into the ground, this would be done after their departure.

Their limousine followed the hearse and the police motorcycle leading the procession. In a display of respect and solidarity Monique knew she'd never see in New York, drivers going in the opposite direction pulled over and turned on their headlights until the last car in the procession had passed.

She felt better after hearing the minister's comforting words, and also from seeing the familiar names of her grandparents and other family members on the surrounding headstones. She gave her mother's hand a reassuring squeeze and was encouraged when her mother squeezed back. They would get through this.

She stood alone, lost in her thoughts, and turned at the feel of a hand on her elbow. "Mac! How nice of you to come." He looked marvelous in a well-fitting charcoal gray suit, royal-blue shirt, and geometric-print tie in black, white, and blue.

"I asked Connie to keep me posted with any news. Are you okay?"

She sighed. "I feel a lot better now that it's over."

"Good. You were so upset last week, I was worried the funeral might be too much for you. How are your parents, especially your mother? Peggy was her sister, right?"

"Yes. They were just a year apart, so you can imagine how close they were. But Mom's handling it well. She's over there talking to a friend." She pointed with her chin.

"I'm glad everyone's coping well."

"I appreciate your concern. Are you coming to the Post? Connie's catering the luncheon, so you know how good the food will be."

"Yes, she rushed off right after the service to start getting ready. I'm sure it'll be great, but I really need to get changed and back to work."

Now that he was here she didn't want him to leave. She took his arm and said in her most convincing voice, "Come join us, Mac. The service didn't run that long, and you've got to eat lunch anyway."

He shrugged and broke into a smile. "All right. I guess I can follow the crowd."

"That's another reason to come," she said, a brilliant smile accenting her words. "There must be at least two hundred people here. Haven't you heard it's bad luck to break a funeral procession?"

The relaxed mood that had begun at the conclusion of the graveside service continued to be displayed by the luncheon attendees. Several volunteers stood poised to serve the buffet luncheon Connie had prepared. Soon mourners' plates were filled with spiral-sliced ham, roast beef, fried sliced potatoes and onions, macaroni and cheese, green beans, and rolls. A jazz CD played softly in the background.

Round cloth-covered tables of ten filled most of the room. Monique circulated, greeting people and accepting condolences, including hugs from Peggy and Teddy's male contemporaries that lasted longer than necessary. After getting yet another disapproving look from a middle-aged wife, she began stepping back from the men and extending her hand instead.

When she was finally able to get a plate she sat at a table with her cousin Liz; Liz's charming teenaged daughter, Adrian; Lyman, Connie, and Mac. Unfortunately, it was too late for her to sit next to Mac, who was sandwiched between Adrian and Lyman.

"This food is just fabulous," Liz was saying. "I don't remember ever having food this good at a funeral. Leave it to Uncle Teddy."

"Connie, it must have taken you forever to do all this cooking," Monique said.

"No, not really. I have a food processor, and that sliced the potatoes, chopped all the onions, and shredded the cheese. The ham was already cooked and just had to be heated. There's nothing to roasting meat. The most involved part was boiling all that macaroni."

"Well, this is definitely the nicest funeral I've ever been to," Lyman said. "Teddy even has an open bar. All they need is dancing and you'd think you were at a wedding."

"He wanted it nice for Peggy," Monique said.

"Wait till they bring out the dessert," Connie said. "The cake is imprinted with a photo of Peggy taken on her wedding day."

"Wow," Liz said. "Did you do that, Connie?"

"No, I just did the food. Teddy ordered all the desserts from the bakery."

From where Monique sat she could see the servers put the chafing dishes away and set up desserts consisting of a variety of cookies, Napoleons and other pastries, brownies, and chocolate-covered strawberries surrounding a large round cake with Peggy's photo. The guests oohed and aahed over the photo, as Peggy had been quite a beauty in her youth and had remained so until her illness.

The crowd began to thin out after dessert. It was Thursday, and many people, like Mac, had to get back to work. Monique listened to people murmuring about how wonderful the food had been, and it jarred something in her memory. Mac had told her how much he'd miss Connie's breakfasts. But those fancier meals didn't start until around the same time he had checked in. Was there a connection? Had Connie set out to impress Mac with her culinary skills?

Monique frowned as she tried to remember Mac's interactions with Connie. He'd asked her to let him know about Peggy's funeral arrangements, so obviously he'd given her his phone number. He'd said she'd told him at the service that she'd done the cooking for the luncheon, so they must have sat together at the church. And he took a seat next to her at the table just a little while ago. If Connie was following the adage that the way to a man's heart was through his stomach, Mac seemed to be responding.

As for Connie, there'd been nothing unusual about her behavior other than that one time, weeks ago, when she seemed agitated when Lyman showed up, for reasons Monique still didn't understand. She'd forgotten about that for the most part, and since that occurred before Mac arrived in Washington, it couldn't have anything to do with him. Nor had Connie said anything about Mac other than a general comment on how nice looking he was, but of course the mood of their breakfasts together became more somber after Peggy went into the hospital for what they knew would be the last time.

A dullness crept into her middle at the thought of giving up her hopes of snaring Mac, but she knew that stepping aside and letting nature take its course was the right thing to do. If Connie wanted Mac she wouldn't interfere. Connie had become a good friend, and friends were hard to come by. It really didn't matter much anyway. It seemed only fitting for Monique to forget about the only man in Washington who didn't show the slightest interest in her.

Except that he was the only man in Washington she had any interest in.

Chapter 12

Fancy That

Things slowly got back to normal following Peggy's funeral. Monique resumed her everyday activities: having breakfast with Connie after the guests had eaten, working out at the spa with Liz, and in between, doing the bookkeeping, supervising the redecoration, and working on her manuscript. And now that it was spring she tinkered in the garden, preparing to do some new landscaping.

"Mmm, smells like pancakes," she said cheerfully one morning upon reaching the kitchen.

"Close," Connie replied. "I made Belgian waffles. Blueberries are optional."

"I hate blueberries," Monique said. "Not only do they stick in my teeth, but they turn them blue. Now I know why you put blueberry syrup on the shopping list." A furrow formed on her forehead. Mac had been gone for over a week. Why was Connie still making these fancy breakfasts?

"Hi, Monique."

She turned at the sound of Lyman's voice. "Hey. I didn't know you were here."

"Yes, I was just washing my hands." He pulled out a chair and sat, rubbing his palms together. "Now I'm ready to eat."

"It's coming," Connie called from the kitchen.

"You're going to miss this job when it's over," Monique teased, taking a chair opposite him.

"I know, but I'm sure enjoying it while it lasts." He smiled at Connie as she placed a plate before him. The Belgian waffle had been dusted with confectioner's sugar and a dollop of blueberries, and Connie had placed bottles of both maple and blueberry syrup on the table.

Monique's mouth inadvertently dropped open as she observed the scene. Something about the way Connie smiled at Lyman as she served him breakfast . . . It was the very definition of infatuation.

In an instant Monique realized Connie hadn't been cooking to get to Mac's heart. It was *Lyman's* heart she was after. Monique's eyes sparkled with the joy of discovery. How could she have missed it? Connie beamed like a high-wattage flashlight as Lyman praised her talent for cooking.

"You like Lyman, don't you, Connie?" she said after Lyman had gone upstairs to work and the two of them were alone.

Connie smiled sheepishly. "Yeah, I do. You don't think it's silly, do you?"

"Of course not. I think it's charming."

"I'm afraid it's all one-sided. Do you have any suggestions for me, Monique? You've been out in the dating world recently." She sighed. "But then again, you don't have any problems attracting men. They all run after you, even the mailman, for heaven's sake."

"Every one except the one I want," she said without thinking.

"Who's that?"

Now it was Monique's turn to look embarrassed, but she decided she could trust Connie with her confidence, just as Connie had trusted her. "Mac."

Connie drew in her breath, and her eyes grew wide. "Oh, Monique, I think that's wonderful. From that first day I met him I thought y'all would make a real good looking couple."

"Yeah, we would, if I could get him to look at me." The field suddenly having cleared hardly meant she was a shoo-in with Mac. For one thing, he was no longer staying at the inn, and she didn't know where he was. She'd commented about his new place when she was checking him out Sunday, hoping he'd tell her about it, but he just named the street it was on. She felt reasonably certain it was his lack of familiarity with Washington rather than deliberate evasiveness that kept him from saying any more. Still, when it came time for him to leave, he'd simply shaken her hand, thanked her, and left, as if he was walking out of her life forever.

To Connie she said, "As I said, every man seems to be running after me except for Mac. When he checked out he didn't express any wish to see me again."

"He came to Peggy's funeral. He gave me the number of his cell phone and asked me to let him know what was going on. He said he was worried about you. That has to stand for something."

"You're sweet, Connie, but honestly, I think he was just trying to be polite. After all, I'd come to his aid that day his truck broke down. We talked a little bit then about how sick Aunt Peggy was, and I'm afraid I wasn't very beguiling. If anything, I was practically crying. He probably thought I was having a nervous breakdown."

"And he took time off from work to come to the

funeral just so he could make sure you were all right. He never knew Peggy, and he barely knew Teddy."

Monique took a moment to consider this. "Actually, he did seem kind of concerned. . . ."

"You see?" Connie said, pouncing on the positive note like a cat racing after catnip. "If he wasn't interested in you at all he would have merely come to the wake Wednesday night, but funerals tend to bring out more emotions in people. Believe me, I know."

Monique knew Connie was thinking about the loss of her husband. Even though she was ready to try love again, the pain of that time would undoubtedly remain with her forever. "Thanks, Connie. You've given me a reason to hope."

Monique squeezed the French bread. It didn't feel as fresh as it should. She didn't want to disappoint Connie, but it looked like she'd have to be satisfied merely making pancakes tomorrow morning. She knew no one would complain.

She checked Connie's list, then headed for the cereal aisle. They always kept several varieties of cereal on hand for those who had willpower strong enough to say no to Connie's breakfasts. While she was in that aisle she'd pick up the pancake syrup Connie needed as well. They went through pancake syrup like households with young children went through milk.

"Monique?"

She turned at the sound of her name, breaking into a smile when she saw who had spoken to her. "Mac! What a nice surprise seeing you here."

"It's good to see you. You're looking well."

"I'm doing pretty good. All of us are. But we miss you at the inn."

"I ran into Lyman the other day at Bill's Hot Dogs. I go there at least twice a week." He smiled at her warmly. "I'm glad I bumped into you. I was going to call you," he said with a hesitation she found charming, adding, "I hope you don't mind."

"I guess that would depend on what it was you were planning to call me."

They laughed, and when Mac spoke again his voice sounded more confident. "My job gives an annual picnic, an Employee Appreciation Day. They invite their employees and their families. My nephew's coming down from Raleigh to spend his spring break with me, so he'll be going. They're having softball and other outdoor games, and there'll be plenty of food and live music. I was wondering if you'd like to come along as my guest."

"Sounds like fun. When is it?"

"Sunday afternoon. I think it runs from twelve to six at Goose Creek Park."

She stole a glimpse at his shopping cart as he spoke. Apparently he was a big fan of the deli. She noticed roast beef and cheese in plastic deli bags, several of those heavy-coated white bags they used for cooked chicken pieces, as well as containers of potato and macaroni salad. "Grocery shopping," she remarked. "One of life's necessary evils, isn't it?"

"The other is cooking," he said. "As you can see, I don't do much of it."

"Neither do I. But if you run a bed-and-breakfast, chances are you're going to spend a fair amount of time in the supermarket, even if someone else does the cooking." She smiled at him, suddenly feeling relaxed and divinely happy. He did want to see her again. Connie's instincts were right. "You have my number, don't you?"

"Yes, I held on to your business card. I'll call you by the weekend."

She thought she heard him make a sound and waited a moment, but when he remained silent she decided she'd imagined it. "Good seeing you, Mac. I'll talk to you in a few days." She moved on.

Mac gripped the handles of his shopping cart tightly. That was a close one. He'd come that close to asking Monique if it would be all right if he called her sooner than the weekend. A sixth sense had stopped him, even though he'd opened his mouth to ask the question.

Most of his contact with other people was limited to working hours. Occasionally he went to have a few beers with the guys after work on Friday, but for the most part when work ended, he went home to a silent apartment. While he had lived alone in Raleigh, he had an active social life, with siblings, nieces, and nephews stopping by to say hello, plus the company of longtime friends and whichever young lady he was dating at the moment. Since he'd been in Washington, most of his contact with his large extended family and his friends was over the phone, and he wasn't seeing anyone romantically.

At work they were so busy trying to catch up for clients displeased with their homes being behind schedule that he'd been working half days on Saturdays, after which he found himself too tired to face the two-hour drive to Raleigh, which he'd only have to repeat the next day to get back. One of his sisters had a key to his house and was checking on it regularly in his absence.

But the lack of human contact was making him lonely. He started to ask Monique if she'd be interested in having dinner with him on Friday, but he quickly decided she might read too much into it. He'd already invited her to the picnic on Sunday, and he wasn't even sure that was a wise move. But she was so easy on his eyes, and she'd looked so vulnerable in the days before her aunt's death, nothing at all like the man-eater he'd pegged her as. Of course, by the day of the funeral she had recovered sufficiently to be back to her cajoling ways, but he really didn't much mind her talking him into staying for the luncheon. It had certainly been an education, as he observed Monique being embraced by one seventyish gentleman after another under the guise of offering her comfort. Even from halfway across the room he could tell the men actually relished holding a young, pretty girl like Monique. To his amusement she actually began to look a little uncomfortable as she tried to discreetly wiggle away, and from then on he noticed she was shaking their hands.

The men in Washington didn't seem to want to leave her alone. First it was the men at the barbershop. Then that dude at the local bar, who unlike the others appeared to be the right age, at least, if somewhat intoxicated, and now the men at the funeral, who were the age of her bereaved uncle.

He decided inviting her to the picnic was a harmless gesture. He couldn't deny that she was in his thoughts constantly, and that whenever he saw her he didn't want to take his eyes off her. He wanted to spend time with her, to learn what she was really like. He'd seen several different sides of her and wanted to know which one was the real Monique. A picnic was a nice, relaxed atmosphere. Surely Monique wouldn't expect too much from it.

On the other hand, she might read too much into a

dinner date. He assured himself he'd done right not to offer an invitation. One more night alone in front of the television wouldn't kill him. His nephew Jerome was arriving by bus Saturday afternoon, and he'd be around for a week. And if he found the silence on Friday night unbearable, he could always slip into a sports coat and go to one of the local nightspots in Greenville, or to the local bar right here in Washington.

Now he understood why the old codger and that young cat hung around the barbershop all day. Too much solitude could be a terrible thing.

Monique realized she was grinning at everyone she saw as she completed her shopping. She forced her lips into a more natural position. A pleasant expression was one thing, but she probably looked like a grinning fool. And what if she ran into Mac again before she checked out? It'd be too embarrassing.

But she was thrilled Mac had invited her out. A company picnic might not be the most sophisticated outing to go on, but it was an afternoon spent with Mac nonetheless. Wait till she told Connie.

Chapter 13

Jitters

Monique rose at her usual seven-thirty the next morning, but she deliberately stayed away from the kitchen. While it certainly was feasible for her to hold a discreet conversation with Connie in the kitchen while the guests ate, Lyman would probably insist upon knowing what they were giggling about, and her news was for Connie's ears only.

She caught up on the morning news and wrote out a few checks. She didn't head for the kitchen until after nine.

"Hey there," Connie said. "I was beginning to think I'd have to eat by myself."

"What'd you make? My nose can't quite place it."

"Huevos rancheros."

Monique wrinkled her nose. "Don't you think it's a little early for tomato products?"

"People drink Bloody Marys with brunch all the time. Besides, didn't you ever have to drink tomato juice with breakfast when you were a kid?"

"Never. My mom only served orange or apple juice."

"What took you so long to get here, anyway?" Connie asked impatiently. "The one day I have great news, you oversleep."

"What's your news?"

"Lyman invited me out!"

Monique jumped up and then hugged Connie, stifling an excited squeal. "That's wonderful! When are you going, and where?"

"Friday night. He asked if I've seen that new romantic comedy everybody's talking about. When I told him I hadn't, he suggested that we go see it Friday, and then he added that while we're out we can go someplace and have somebody cook for me for a change."

"I'm so happy for you, Connie. And you're very lucky, because it's not every man who's willing to see what's generally regarded as a chick flick. In fact, Liz and I are seeing it Friday, too. But we'll probably see a later show than you and Lyman. She and I are eating before the movie. When you're on a date you usually eat after." She watched as Connie's smile dissolved. "What's wrong? Even if we see the same show and bump into you, we won't say anything to embarrass you."

"It's not that. It's just that I'm kind of nervous, Monique. I've known Lyman most of my life—I had a crush on him in high school, years before I even met my husband—but it's been years since I've been on a date. I don't even know what to wear."

"Something casual, definitely. Slacks and a sweater. And don't be nervous. Dates haven't changed much. You've got an advantage in that you know specifically what his plans are. A dinner date can mean L'Auberge, or it can mean Bill's Hot Dogs."

"You're exaggerating."

"Just trying to get my point across. Relax. You'll have fun."

"I'm sure I will."

"Well, I've got some news myself. I ran into Mac at

the Piggly Wiggly, and he asked if I'd go with him to the picnic his job is giving Sunday."

Now it was Connie's turn to envelop Monique in a bear hug. "See, what'd I tell you?"

"Yes, you were right, and I'm glad. I'm feeling a little guilty, though. I broke a promise I made to myself."

"You mean like the promise you made to stop smoking?" Connie said, with a disapproving look at Monique's cigarette.

"Yeah, that too. But I promised myself no more men." At Connie's shocked expression she rushed on. "No, I don't mean forever. It's just that every time I get involved with someone it's so beautiful in the beginning, and then it all goes down the toilet. I've realized that the blame generally rests with me, and I don't want it to happen anymore."

"Oh, I wouldn't worry about that. Just relax and be comfortable," Connie said, "and you should be all right. Like I told you before, from the minute I met Mac I thought he'd be a good match for you. But you didn't really seem interested when I felt you out, so I let it drop. Little did I know you were having the same idea. If anything, I thought you were interested in Lyman."

"Lyman!"

Connie shrugged. "It's not like you discouraged him when he'd flirt with you."

Suddenly Monique understood the reason for Connie's near-hostile behavior when Lyman was around. "Only because I considered him harmless, just like Uncle Teddy's friends always telling me they want to take me out," she explained. "Of course, Lyman's not an old-timer, but he's not my type. But how do you like this—I thought you were making all those fancy breakfasts for Mac."

"You didn't!"

"It didn't hit me until later that Lyman started work just before Mac checked in." They giggled like six-year-olds, and then Monique sighed dreamily. "Now I feel like Cupid shot an arrow at me, and it went straight to my heart."

"You know things rarely happen exactly when we're ready for them to happen," Connie pointed out. "Like pregnancy, for example. Who among us can say we were actually planned?"

"Yeah, so I've heard," Monique replied wistfully. Then she brightened. "So are you going to call me on Saturday and tell me all about your date with Lyman, did you want to get together on Sunday, or would you rather wait until Monday morning?"

"Oh, I think it'll be more fun if we wait until Monday. I'll fix a nice breakfast, and we can sit and exchange our stories."

"Great. But, Connie, please, nothing with tomato sauce, eh?"

Monique was working on the inn's books when the phone began to ring. She picked it up promptly and gave her standard professional greeting, identifying the B&B for the caller and offering assistance.

"Hi, Monique, it's Mac."

"Hi, Mac!"

"I meant to tell you, you really sound great answering the phone."

She laughed. "Thanks. I think when I leave here I'll probably still answer the phone by identifying my apartment as the Dodson Bed-and-Breakfast."

After a few seconds of silence he asked, "Are you planning on leaving?"

"Well, certainly not right away. But my home base is in Atlanta. I came up to help Uncle Teddy out because he was so busy with Aunt Peggy. Actually, when I came up I didn't expect her to leave us so quickly. I guess I need to talk to my uncle. Now that she's gone he may want to take over."

"And if he does, would you go back to Atlanta?"

"I really don't know. My job was eliminated at the end of last year. I'm not sure if I'd go there or back to New York, but since I don't have a job I'd probably go to Atlanta just long enough to get my things, then go to New York and stay with my parents while I get my career back on track."

"I guess that'd be the most sensible thing to do. By the way, I was calling to make sure we're still on for Sunday."

"Oh, yes. I'm looking forward to it. You said about noon, right?"

"Yes. My nephew comes in from Raleigh tomorrow afternoon. I hope he has a good time while he's here, since I'll be at work during the day. You know how kids are. It would help if I knew someone his age I could introduce him to."

"How old did you say he was?"

"Seventeen. He'll be graduating from high school soon."

"I have a cousin around that age, maybe a little younger. She's a high school junior. You met her at the Post after Aunt Peggy's funeral. Her mother's my cousin, too."

"Oh, yes, I remember. Your cousin was there with her daughter." He had immediately recognized Monique's cousin Liz as the woman accompanying Monique that night at the neighborhood bar when he thought she was out with the mailman. Bringing the daughter along might not be a bad idea. He remembered her being a cute little thing, and Jerome was sure to like her. "Do you think she'd want to come?"

"I don't see a problem, except she might not be ready that early. She sings in the church choir, so she's at worship every Sunday."

"That's all right. It goes on till six, so if we don't get there until one, it's not like they'll run out of food. Why don't you ask her?"

"I'll do that. Mac, I just realized I don't have your number."

"I actually use my cell exclusively. It's going to be a long-distance number, because it's from Raleigh," he said apologetically.

"No problem. I'll use my cell to call you." She took his number down and promised to get back to him about Adrian.

As Monique dressed for her evening out with Liz, she couldn't help wondering if Mac had any plans for the evening. Was he going to one of the clubs in Greenville that featured a more mature crowd? It didn't matter, she told herself. *She* was the one he'd invited to the company picnic.

Still, she couldn't help wondering if he'd go out and possibly meet someone else. Maybe she should have agreed when Liz suggested they go to a club tonight. There was a time when she went out dancing every chance she got, but that had been a long time ago. Her interests had changed as she got older, and now a little dancing once in a while was plenty. She'd successfully talked Liz into having dinner and seeing a movie instead.

It hadn't been easy. Liz's two main goals in life seemed to be having a good time and finding a second husband, in that order. She hated to waste a Friday night going to the movies where she wasn't likely to meet anyone new. Monique noted wryly that the husband-hunting Liz was an unlikely companion for her because of her self-imposed hiatus from the male species.

She didn't consider herself having broken her vow. All she was doing was getting her feet wet, easing back into the company of a man.

Because a picnic really wasn't a *date*. . . .

Chapter 14

Be Careful What You Wish For . . .

Connie soaked amid chest-deep bubbles in the luxurious sculpted bathtub. The investment she and Charles had made in updating their home's master bathroom had been a wise choice. Not only had it raised the value of the house, but she felt like Queen Nefertiti when she bathed. Some things you just couldn't put a price on.

As she ran the washcloth up her left arm she noticed the still-pale strip of skin on her fourth finger, which up until recently had been covered by her engagement and wedding rings. It had never occurred to her to remove them, the symbols of her marriage to Charles, in all the long months since his untimely death from a heart attack. But when she became reacquainted with Lyman Watkins when he began working on remodeling the bed-and-breakfast, something had stirred in her. She'd recognized the feeling, in spite of its having been years since she'd last felt it. She was attracted to Lyman, her old crush from high school. She was widowed, he was divorced, and over thirty years had passed since high school, but she felt girlish and giddy, as if she were fourteen years old all over again.

At first she felt terribly guilty for removing her rings,

as if she were somehow being disloyal to her late husband. In twenty-one years of marriage she'd never been drawn to another man, had never, as Jimmy Carter so famously said, lusted in her heart for anyone other than Charles. The most she'd done was express admiration for a good-looking man, almost always from a distance, like on television or the movie screen. There'd been no shortage of handsome male celebrities to enjoy looking at. Most of them were younger, like Michael Jordan, George Clooney, and Morris Chestnut; but others were her age or older, proof that advancing age wasn't synonymous with losing one's appeal. Skye Audsley from that TV news magazine show *A Day in the Life* was well into his forties. Denzel was close to fifty, and Richard Gere past fifty.

Charles had been gone for over a year now. Sometimes, when she woke up after a particularly deep sleep, she actually forgot. She'd cast a groggy look at the other side of the bed and think to herself that he was already up and that she had to get going herself to fix him breakfast before he headed off to his job as manager of a men's clothing store in Greenville. A few times she'd actually sat up and swung her legs to the side of the bed when her head would suddenly clear and she would remember that awful day last year when Arthur Winston called her from the golf course. He and Charles had been relaxing after completing eighteen holes when Charles suddenly slumped over. The paramedics had been called promptly, but Connie learned later it was already too late. The massive attack had killed him instantly.

She raised the drain closer with her big toe and watched the water level decrease until the last of it swirled down the drain, along with the remainder of the bubbles. She stood up and turned on the shower, picking up the handheld shower head for a thorough rinse.

In spite of what Monique had said about dating not having changed a lot since she'd done it last, she felt apprehensive. *This is silly,* she told herself as she stepped out of the tub. *You've wanted this for weeks, and now that it's happened you're wondering if you did the right thing in accepting.* She'd spent many a morning sharing easy conversation over breakfast with Lyman. He'd been almost shy when he asked her if she'd consider going out with him. She accepted but didn't tell him this would be her first date since Charles died; she suspected he already knew but didn't want to ask. He was that kind of guy.

What Lyman *didn't* know was that she'd been crazy about him in high school. He'd been a senior when she was a freshman. Their respective grade levels and the corresponding age difference between a fourteen-year-old and a seventeen-year-old were as far apart as Jupiter and Pluto, and he never even spoke to her, never knew how she worshipped him from a distance. After he graduated and went to college she'd fastened her attentions to another fellow, someone closer to her own age, and this time the object of her affections felt the same way about her. After college she met Charles, fell in love, and married him.

She'd seen Lyman many times over the years. The social circle in a town the size of Washington was rather small, and she and Charles had many mutual friends, including Diane and Arthur Winston. Arthur had been playing golf with Charles the day he died, and Connie had worked with Diane to coordinate school activities—Diane's daughter was just a year younger than Glenn. Connie had occasionally laughed to herself when she remembered how crazy she'd been about Lyman, but most of the time she didn't even think about it.

But now she couldn't help considering the irony of her girlhood dream coming true after so many years.

She was dressed a full fifteen minutes before Lyman was due to arrive. Like Monique had suggested, she dressed casually, in a long, hip-hiding cable-knit sweater and slacks. Her hair looked fine—she'd had the gray covered with a rinse—and her makeup freshly applied. Only one thing remained for her to do, something so difficult she'd deliberately postponed it as long as she could.

As she lifted the framed picture of herself and Charles from the fireplace mantel she kept reminding herself that she'd survived the equally traumatic removal of her engagement and wedding rings. *You can do this, too,* she told herself over and over again.

She looked lovingly at the photograph. To celebrate their twentieth anniversary they had taken a cruise to the Virgin Islands, and they had a photograph taken the final night at dinner. Charles looked so handsome in his black suit and silver shirt and tie.

Again she felt a pang of guilt stabbing at her chest. She didn't quite understand her emotions. Surely Charles wouldn't have wanted her to shrivel up and sever herself from the world. He'd been a loving, giving man she'd been blessed to have as her husband for over twenty years. But now that he was gone and she was dating . . . well, it simply wouldn't do for Lyman to be greeted with a picture from her past.

Connie closed her eyes, holding the picture to her chest. "I'll never forget you, Charles," she whispered.

Opening her eyes, she lowered the photograph and carried it to the spare room, where she placed it on top of a bookcase. Perhaps a day would come when she'd feel it necessary to put it in Glenn's room or pack it away entirely, but for now this spot, away from the sight of the casual visitor, would do fine.

"That was a fun movie," Connie said as she and Lyman emerged from the theater.

"Yeah, it wasn't bad at all," he agreed. "But that long scene when they were talking in a moving car was ridiculous. All these people who drive in the movies should be dead. None of them ever looks at the road."

"I've noticed that, too. I don't know why the directors still allow actors to focus on their passenger instead of where they're going in those driving scenes. It looks so phony."

"I should have been a film director," Lyman said. "You'd never see anybody fall into a pool, get soaking wet, and be dry in the next shot in any movie *I* made."

"Oh, I've seen that happen lots of times," she said, laughing. "I've heard people behind me whispering, 'No way could he get dry that fast.'"

"I'm glad you enjoyed it, Connie." Lyman unlocked the doors to his Pathfinder as they approached. He opened her door and helped her climb in. "Now let's get ourselves something to eat."

Connie had the uneasy feeling that all her neighbors were watching Lyman seat her in the Pathfinder when he picked her up. When they returned to her home nearly four hours later she had the same wariness. Were they timing how long she'd been gone? Would they wait to see how much time elapsed before he came out? And how long would it take for the news that she'd been out with a man to travel to every resident of the block?

Her hand shook as she unlocked the front door.

"You want me to do that?" Lyman offered.

"Oh, no, thanks. I guess I'm not accustomed to being out at night."

He followed her inside. "Don't be nervous, Connie."

"Nervous?" She'd intended to laugh it off, but the squeaky way her voice came out made that impossible. Had that Minnie Mouse squeal actually come from her throat? "All right, so maybe I am a little."

He reached out and rested a hand on each of her shoulders. "Don't be. I've been divorced fourteen years, but I know this is all new to you. I just wanted to see you safely inside and thank you for going out with me." His voice took on the shy, almost childlike quality she found so endearing. "I hope you had as much fun as I did."

"I had a wonderful time, Lyman," she said sincerely.

He broke into the broad grin she'd always found so appealing, even when he was a teenager. "Good. We'll do it again, huh?"

"I'd love to." Inwardly she cringed at her choice of words. *Listen to yourself, Connie! 'I had a wonderful time.' 'I'd love to.' Can't you think of something original? He'll think you're completely insincere.*

"Good. In the meantime I'll see you Monday at work." His hands still on her shoulders, he leaned in and kissed her left cheek. He was gone before she could find her voice.

She stood in the doorway as he walked to his vehicle, and when he waved just before pulling off she waved back. She closed the door, a satisfied smile covering her face. How considerate Lyman was. He hadn't even kissed her on the mouth because he felt it might make her uncomfortable.

Her lips remained curved in a smile as she climbed the stairs leading to her bedroom. After the most difficult period she'd ever had to face, life had just reminded her how wonderful it could really be.

Chapter 15

Sunday in the Park With Mac

Bright sunshine worked its way through Monique's bedroom blinds on Sunday morning. She quickly dressed and went to the kitchen, where she sautéed green pepper and ham to be used in western omelets. Two of the guest rooms were occupied by a total of four people, but no one had come down yet. She ventured outside and picked up the Sunday paper, then sat down in the living room and read it while she waited.

Breakfast on Saturdays and Sundays was served an hour later than on weekdays, from eight to ten. Even if no one came down until the last minute, she still had plenty of time to load the dishwasher, straighten up the kitchen, and shower, wash her hair, and dress. Mac wasn't picking her up until one because Adrian was attending church service this morning.

After much thought she decided to dress casually, remembering what Mac said about softball. A little exercise would do her good, since she hadn't gotten to the spa yesterday or Friday. Still, dressing casually didn't mean she should look like a slob. She wanted to look good.

* * *

Mac watched with a mixture of amusement and admiration. Monique hit that softball as if it were an enemy coming to kill her, then sprinted toward first base as the outfielders tried unsuccessfully to catch the powerful ball.

When he picked her up he'd been pleased to see she wore shorts and gym shoes. He and Jerome had both worn polo shirts and jeans. Of course, he'd told Monique it was a picnic, but he drew the line at suggesting that she dress casually. By her own admission she was forty years old, and if she didn't know by now what was appropriate attire for a picnic she never would. Still, he half expected her to emerge from the B&B overdressed—like some of the women here who looked ridiculous walking around the park in dresses and high heels—only to take one look at his casual attire and go back in to change.

He knew she worked out regularly, so he expected her to be shapely under those loose-fitting sweatpants she usually wore. But there was a difference between working out and being athletic. When Monique ran she was as graceful as a gazelle, her arms bent at the elbows and moving back and forth, not flailing about wildly like those of some of the other women in the game. Yes, the more he saw of Monique Oliver, the more he liked.

A male player who took to the bat while Monique was on second base hit a home run, allowing Monique to run to third and then to home. Mac applauded, his hands held over his head, while Jerome and Adrian, standing at his side, cheered.

He inadvertently licked his lips at the sight of Monique running toward him. She moved easily, her breasts firm, her bent arms moving in symmetry with her legs. His gaze lingered on her lower limbs. Funny.

Monique was small, but she wasn't slim. She possessed what was known in the vernacular as big legs, shapely and sizable, and he was suddenly grateful she'd worn shorts. He'd always been a leg man. He just hoped she wouldn't notice that he couldn't take his eyes off hers.

"Great hit," he said as they took turns slapping raised palms.

"Thanks."

"Hey, Mac, you're up!"

He grabbed a bat and stood poised over home plate. He suddenly felt a little nervous. What if he struck out? Maybe it was silly in this day and age, but it would be a little embarrassing to be bested by a woman, especially one who was his date. His anxiety only increased as he refused the first ball the pitcher threw, and then the second. Only by telling himself this was a game, not a competition, was he able to hit the third ball. It practically sailed into the mitt of the first baseman.

His team members voiced a collective moan as he sheepishly made his way back to the dugout. "I knew I shouldn't have hit that ball," he said regretfully to Monique.

"Oh, these things happen," she said cheerfully. "I wouldn't worry about it if I were you."

Jerome spoke up. "Uncle Mac, is it okay if Adrian and me take a boat out?"

"Sure. Just make sure you wear your life jackets."

"Okay. See you later!"

Mac and Monique watched as the teens rushed toward the waterfront.

"They seem to be getting along pretty well," she remarked.

"Yes, and I'm glad. He must have asked me fifty times if I was sure she was cute."

"Well, you know how kids are. They're always suspicious of adults' motives, and they tend to be on the shallow side. They outgrow it." She paused a beat, then softly added, "Usually."

He wondered what her last remark was all about.

They resumed the game, and Mac, in the outfield, made several good catches. Their team managed to win by a hair. When it came time for the three-legged race, Monique paired with Adrian and Mac with Jerome. Never before had Mac felt so clumsy. He and Jerome had only gone a few steps when they fell on the grass, literally tripping over their own feet that shared a burlap sack. Mac angrily jerked his foot out of the sack and then focused on both Monique and Adrian, who were jerkily but steadily making their way toward the finish line. They finished in third place.

"I guess you and I should have practiced," he said to Jerome.

"Ah, who cares about a three-legged race anyway?"

But Mac knew his nephew was just as embarrassed as he was at having been beaten by Monique and Adrian.

In between games they ate hot dogs, hamburgers, chicken, and corn on the cob, bringing their plates to the picnic tables and listening to the live band perform mostly easy-listening numbers.

The final event of the day was the egg toss, for which the organizers had plenty of paper towels and Wet Wipes on hand. "There's a trick to doing this," Mac said to Monique. "You have to throw it gently, of course, but it's also in the way you catch it. Try to cup it gently rather than catch it like a ball." He demonstrated with his hands.

She glanced at the long line of employees and guests who stood opposite each other. "I can see why they saved this game for last. Something tells me this field is going to be a mess before this is over."

"They're expecting rain on Tuesday, so at least the eggs will wash away before they begin to smell."

The game coordinator instructed the participants to stand facing each other with two feet between them. Assistants handed out eggs, and at the coordinator's command they were tossed. A full 20 percent of the catchers had eggs break apart in their hands, and Mac sympathized with the disgust in their facial expressions. He'd never held a raw egg in his hands before, but he imagined it was similar to that mucusy feeling he had when he had a cold and sneezed onto his hand. It wasn't pleasant.

"All right, all remaining contestants move back one foot," the coordinator said through a megaphone.

Now it was Mac's turn to throw to Monique. She cupped her hands and let the egg fall into her palms. When she caught it she leaned her head back and breathed out heavily through her mouth, and Mac realized she'd been holding her breath.

Another group of contestants was eliminated from a field increasingly littered with broken eggs, and those who remained were instructed to step back again. Mac felt apprehensive as he surveyed the approximate six feet that now separated them. The rules of the game dictated that he couldn't move his feet, but he could lean his body forward to shrink the distance, and that's what he did.

Monique caught the egg.

Now only seven or eight teams remained in place, some eight feet apart. "We might as well try tossing it clear across the Pamlico," Monique said, cupping her hands around her mouth to amplify her voice, as if they were standing on the opposite sides of the river. The assistants handed out more eggs, and she leaned forward and tossed hers carefully.

It broke apart in his hand.

"Oh, Mac, I'm so sorry," she said, coming to him as he tried to shake the clinging residue off his hands.

"Not your fault. Hey, hurry up with those napkins, will you?" he called to the employee.

Monique glanced up and down the row and saw people attempting to shake eggs off their hands. "I think everybody's out with that toss. Wait a minute. Oh, they have a winner!"

Mac gratefully accepted paper towels from the assistant. "This isn't helping much. I still feel a film on my hands."

"Someone's coming with a Wet Wipe."

Jerome and Adrian came to stand by them. "You're brave, Uncle Mac," Jerome said. "I wasn't about to get that mess all over my hands."

"You guys did real good," Adrian added. "I think they're giving out some kind of gift certificate to those who got as far as you guys did."

"Good job, Mac," the coordinator said when he stood next to him. He held out an envelope. "We've got gift certificates to Chili's in Greenville for each team who got to the last round."

"Oh, how nice," Monique said.

"I wonder what the winners got," Adrian mused aloud.

"Monique, you take it," Mac said. "I've got to get this gunk off my hands."

The coordinator held out the box of wipes for Mac to pull from. "Thank you for coming. We hope you had a good time."

"Yeah, I had a lot of fun," Jerome said, expressing a sentiment shared by all four of them.

Monique wasn't surprised when Mac dropped Adrian off first. She turned discreetly away as Jerome walked her to the front door, but Mac kept his eye on them. "Don't you think you should give them a little privacy?" she asked.

"Heck, no. Hmm. Holding hands . . . a kiss on the cheek. Something tells me Jerome's not gonna be lonely this week."

"I think it's awful the way you're looking at them," she hissed.

"Oops. Here he comes. I don't want him to catch me looking." He reached out for her shoulder and pulled her closer to him. Before she could ask what was going on, his lips were on hers, taking full advantage of the fact that her mouth had been poised to ask a question by plunging his tongue inside. She closed her eyes and enjoyed the light-headed sensation from the unexpected action, but the kiss was practically over before it began. The sound of a throat being cleared grounded her instantly, and she reluctantly pulled back.

"Am I interrupting something?" Jerome asked, his voice tinged with amusement.

"Mind your business, Jerome," Mac warned good-naturedly. He steered the Explorer out onto the road. In just a few minutes they were in front of the bed-and-breakfast. "I'll be right back," he said to Jerome.

Monique said good-bye to Jerome, and then she and Mac made their way up the front walk. His hand rested lightly on her shoulder. The sky was cloaked in the brilliant sunshine that occurred in the early stages of sunset. "Thanks for inviting me along, Mac," she said. "I had fun. So did Adrian, I'm sure."

"I can't take credit for that. That was your idea. But I'm glad both of you came. Jerome and I enjoyed the day much better because you two were with us." He glanced at the window while she unlocked the door. "Do you have any guests?"

"We did, but both couples checked out this morning. No one is scheduled to arrive until Tuesday, and that's just one person." She pushed the door open and went in, Mac following close behind. "But by the end of next week we'll have three rooms. We're starting to get into our busy sea—"

Her words were lost as he swiftly moved to kiss her again. The door was closed behind them, and no one could see inside. This time there would be no interruptions reminding them someone was watching, because no one was.

She'd dreamed of kissing him this way, with all the hunger her healthy woman's body had stored for so long. The kiss they shared in the truck was just a teaser; this was the real thing. She stood on tiptoe, her arms reaching around his neck, stretching her body like a lithe cat, burrowing closer to him, her tongue intertwined with his in the most sensuous of slow dances. She answered his moans with little sounds of her own, wanting it to go on forever. . . .

Good heavens, what was she doing? This wasn't a romantic dream, it was the real thing; and she was being entirely too easy. What would he think? She backed away from him.

He looked at her through heavy-lidded eyes. "I almost forgot Jerome's waiting in the truck. I'm glad one of us has good sense."

Yeah, one of us. She felt too embarrassed to look him in the eye. "Good night, Mac."

"G'night."

Monique discreetly stood at the window and watched him leave. His step had a jaunty spring to it. The window was closed, but she imagined him whistling a happy tune. And why not? By kissing him with such uncontrolled ardor, she'd practically told him she was willing to be his bed partner while he was here in town.

It would be a difficult impression to erase.

Chapter 16

When the Cat's Away

Monique turned on her car's ignition and was backing out of the driveway when she suddenly remembered she'd borrowed a pair of bike shorts from Liz the other night when she found a tear in hers. Monique was fighting a case of the sniffles and didn't plan on going to work out tonight. In fact, after she ran her errands she was just going to return home and take it easy the rest of the day. Then she remembered that Adrian was out of school this week for spring break. Since she'd already washed Liz's shorts, she might as well drop them off to Adrian in case Liz needed them. Monique knew Liz had her eye on a cute guy who had recently joined the spa.

She stopped at Liz's house first, parking in front of the blue wood-frame cottage with its inviting front porch. The front door was open, the locked screen door allowing air to circulate. She could hear the living room television playing.

Monique rapped on the metal edge of the door. "Adrian, you there?"

"Coming."

The teen, wearing shorts, a striped shirt, and white socks, unlatched the screen door. "Hi, Aunt Monique! I didn't know you were coming over."

"I didn't come to visit. I just wanted to drop these off

to your mother. Will you give them to her for me?" Monique's voice sounded deeper and huskier than usual because of her congestion.

"Sure. You got a cold?"

"I'm trying to get one, yes. I'm going to the post office; then I'll stop at the store and get some soup." The sound of male laughter from inside startled her. "Is there someone here?"

"Oh, that's just Jerome. He's been over every day."

Monique frowned. "Does your mother know that?"

"Sure. It's not like he's here all day, Aunt Monique. He usually comes over about one, and we go out. Today we're going to play miniature golf in Greenville. The only reason he's here this early is that Mom rented a video last night, and I wanted him to watch it with me."

"Adrian, come on! You're missing it," Jerome called from inside.

"I see. Well, you two have a good time. I'll see you later."

"Okay, Aunt Monique. I hope you feel better. 'Bye!"

Monique didn't like the idea of Adrian entertaining Jerome or any boy without an adult being in the house. She certainly hadn't been allowed to do that when *she* was in high school, and she knew Liz hadn't, either. Of course, the rule had been much easier to enforce because neither of their mothers held full-time jobs while they were growing up. Monique attributed the explosion in teen pregnancy to kids being left more on their own. Liz was a single parent, and with her ex-husband currently stationed in Thailand, his contribution to Adrian's upbringing was mostly financial. He was simply too far away to be of much emotional assistance.

Monique's concerns weren't long-lasting—she simply felt too lousy to linger on it—but the subject came up when she picked up Liz on Thursday to drive to the spa.

"I'm so glad you offered to drive," Liz said. "This car is so much more hip than my Taurus."

"You can drive if you want to."

"Nah. I don't want to give the wrong impression. If Cornel asks me out, he'll find out this isn't really my car."

Monique shrugged. "As they say, honesty is the best policy." Something about that line made her think of what she'd seen this afternoon. She quickly realized it was the word "honesty." Maybe she could find out if Liz knew Jerome was in her house while she was at work. "Hey, how's Adrian enjoying her vacation?"

"She likes it a lot more now that Jerome is here. She's been spending practically every minute with him."

"I know he was there the other day when I returned your shorts," Monique said. "They were watching a video in the living room, and the front door was open. Still, it made me a little uncomfortable. I wasn't sure if you knew he was spending time with Adrian while you were at work."

"Oh, sure, I knew. Usually he just comes and gets her, and they go out. When I call in the afternoons there's never any answer."

Monique didn't reply, but she found Liz's explanation unsatisfactory. How could Jerome pick Adrian up when he didn't have a car? She doubted Mac would allow his seventeen-year-old nephew to drive his late-model Explorer. Adrian, on the other hand, drove a nine-year-old silver Toyota, a gift from her father when she'd gotten her license. It would have made a lot more sense for Adrian to drive over to Mac's apartment, pick up Jerome, and then head to their destination from there.

Monique felt Liz was being gullible. Just because Adrian wasn't answering the phone in the afternoons didn't mean she wasn't there. But Monique felt it wasn't her place to point that out, so she kept quiet.

At the spa Monique set about her workout regimen, starting with walking for fifteen minutes at a brisk pace on the treadmill. She glanced over at Liz, who was making a halfhearted attempt at pedaling a stationary bicycle. She smiled. Good thing Liz had inherited the small bone structure of her mother, for she really didn't come here to exercise. She came to socialize, and she wasn't alone. Monique marveled at how little difference there was between an exercise club and a singles bar.

As she trotted on the moving surface beneath her feet, a bearded man with eyes she could only describe as shifty openly looked her up and down, lingering on her ample backside. "You got a license for that trailer?" he drawled.

She made no attempt to disguise rolling her eyes. Lothario here probably thought he was being charming, but she had news for him. Making wisecracks about her anatomy would hardly endear him to her. Monique had not been blessed with the petite frame of the women on her mother's side of the family, but the more chunky build of the Olivers. Working out on a regular basis had become routine to her over the years.

The pesky man soon realized his line had failed, and he moved on, presumably to try it on another woman with wide hips.

As Monique left the treadmill to give her arms a workout on the rowing machine, another man she passed said, "Hey there, Legs." She sucked her teeth, but only after she had passed him and he couldn't hear. All these smooth-talking types flaunting their impressive muscle-laden forms only made her wonder what Mac was doing.

Mac bent forward slightly, hands on hips, breathing heavily. Playing basketball with Jerome had left him winded, and on top of that, he'd lost the best two out of three. He supposed there came a time in every middle-aged man's life when he lost to someone younger and more agile, but just because it happened to everyone sooner or later didn't make it any easier to accept its happening to him.

But Jerome was ecstatic. "The best man, the best man," he gloated, raising arms with hands clasped to one side, then the other.

"All right, all right, so you beat me. How about going to get some dinner? We'll pick up some takeout so we can just bring it home without having to clean up first."

"Taco Bell?"

"If you don't mind your stomach screaming at you in a few hours, sure. I want something from Subway, myself. But we can stop at both places."

They got into the truck. "Uncle Mac, are we going back to Raleigh Saturday or Sunday?" Jerome asked.

"Saturday. Our whole family is going to attend Easter services on Sunday, remember?"

"Uh . . . I guess I forgot. I was hoping we'd drive back on Sunday so I can take Adrian out Saturday night."

"You'll have to make it Friday night. This is the first weekend I haven't had to work since I've been here, and that's only because it's Easter. Who knows when I'll get another two full days off? Every time we get caught up it rains for two days. I'm not missing the chance to sleep in my own bed on Saturday. I know the last day of your school vacation is Easter Monday, but I've got to work that day."

"Oh, maaaaan. I was hoping we'd go back on Sunday."

"Stop whining. I'll give you the certificate I got from my job at the picnic, so you can take Adrian to Chili's on Friday. How's that?"

Jerome brightened instantly. "That'll work. But didn't you give it to Monique?"

"She left it in the truck. I didn't expect her to, but I guess she wanted me to have it. She probably felt that since it was my job who gave the picnic I should keep the certificate."

"If she gave it back to you she's probably expecting you to use it on her."

Mac didn't entirely disagree with his nephew's logic, but he didn't feel it would be right for him to say so. Besides, for all he knew Monique really was just trying to be nice. "Why, because I invited her to the picnic?"

"You wouldn't have asked her if you didn't like her, right?"

"I do like her, Jerome, but we're not joined at the hip." Maybe not, but she was on his brain. He'd had a stirring memory of their good-night kiss just a minute ago, when he spoke about sleeping in his own bed. How much more exciting it would be if she were with him. The blatant hunger she displayed startled him, and he in turn had allowed himself to get equally carried away. He'd thought about her all week, but he'd been too busy, between work during the day and entertaining Jerome in the evening. Besides, Monique had clearly been embarrassed when she broke the kiss, so not hounding her for another date would probably ease any fears she might have about him being anxious to get her into bed.

Okay, so he *was* anxious to get her into bed, but he would never try to use her. He'd had one or two sex-only relationships in his life where it was okay with both him and the lady involved, but Monique simply wasn't that type of woman. She'd probably shown such passion out of mere humanity . . . it might have been as long a time for her as it had been for him. This was just another side of her. He'd seen several sides of her already, the sly side who asked carefully constructed questions to learn about his personal life; the considerate side, genuinely concerned about his welfare after his truck broke down; the sensitive side, so upset by her aunt's terminal illness; the athletic side who could hit and run with the best of them, and the amorous side whose kisses could bring out the beast in a man. The latter aspect piqued his interest the most, his nature if not his intellect, but still lurking in the background was the I'm-fine-and-I-know-it side. In his experience these types were prone to presume after two or three dates that they were in a relationship. He'd been forced to break it off with a few women he'd known who acted that way. It had been disappointing for them both to end what had been a promising alliance.

The older he got, the more aware he became of women's anxieties to establish a lasting romantic relationship, probably because they were older, too. Monique was forty, and women that age knew these were their last years to settle down and have children, if they were ever going to. He could empathize with them, but he wasn't particular about having his own kids. He played such a prominent role as loving uncle and surrogate dad to his nieces and nephews that fatherhood simply wasn't a priority for him.

But when it came to Monique, he'd gladly risk disappointment for another one of those kisses. He'd call her after he got back from Raleigh.

Chapter 17

People Will Talk

Monique and Connie sat down to breakfast. Connie had made pancakes this morning, and Monique piled four on her plate. Still, she knew she'd be going back for seconds. Connie's pancakes were absolutely heavenly. "I'll have to add time to my workout tonight," she said, adding, "but these are so good it's worth it."

"Well, thank you." Connie usually kept up with her, but today her plate held only two pancakes and two strips of bacon.

"What's with you? Are you dieting or something?" Monique asked.

"Sort of. Since I've been dating Lyman I've become more aware of these extra fifty pounds I'm carrying."

"He didn't mention it to you!" Monique said in an accusatory, how-dare-he tone.

"No. I'm sure he's got too much class to mention it. Besides, he's a few pounds overweight himself, in case you hadn't noticed."

"I'd noticed." Monique felt a twinge of disloyalty. Whenever she saw a heavyset couple like Connie and Lyman, she couldn't help imagining a groaning, sagging mattress struggling to support them while they were in the throes of passion, and Connie and Lyman were no exception to the long-standing illusion.

"I think it's unrealistic of me to expect to get down to the recommended weight for my height and age, but I think twenty or twenty-five pounds is doable," Connie continued. "My doctor was thrilled to hear it. She gave me a diet to follow. I actually started cutting down the first time Lyman asked me out, but I didn't make too much of an effort. I'm really serious about it now. You should have heard Glenn tease me about it when he was home last week."

"I'd like to meet your son. You talk about him so much."

"That's because he's my baby. I'm so proud of him. He'll be at the dance the church is giving. You know, the spring social."

"I hadn't heard about it this year yet, but I guess it's about that time."

"I'm going with Lyman. But even Glenn is coming to town for it."

"I'm glad he's not upset that you're dating."

"If anything, he's glad. He worries about me being alone too much. But there's something that worries me that I wanted to talk to you about, Monique."

"What's that?"

They were alone in the dining room, but Connie whispered anyway. "Sex."

Monique could just stare at her. What could she possibly tell Connie, who'd been married for over twenty years, that she didn't know already?

"Specifically, sex in the new millennium. Are there any hard and fast rules, other than to use protection? I've only . . . known my husband for so many years . . . it's embarrassing."

"Don't be embarrassed. That's the only rule I can think of."

"How long should I wait before . . . ?" Connie cleared her throat delicately.

"There's no rule about that. Of course, preferably not the first date, but I know you and Lyman have already been out several times. I guess the best thing I can tell you is to go with your instincts."

"My instincts tell me it's going to happen pretty soon. But it's not as simple as it sounds. Glenn may be away at school, but I don't want my neighbors seeing Lyman's car parked in front of my house all night. You know how people talk. They're already buzzing about me going out with Lyman."

"I know. All I can suggest is that he not stay all night. Your only other option is going to one of the hotels in Greenville." Monique hastily wiped her mouth when the phone started ringing. She got up and picked up the kitchen extension. "Dodson's Bed-and-Breakfast . . . Well, hello, Mac! Yes, I'm fine . . . Easter was pleasant, thank you. Did Jerome get home safely? Oh, how nice."

Connie came into the kitchen and was silently mouthing something to her. With a frown Monique waved her off and turned away. "I'm sure you had a good time. It was your first time back home since you came to Washington, wasn't it? . . . Yes, I understand. I'll talk to you soon. Bye."

"What was all that miming about?" she said as she rejoined Connie at the table.

"I was trying to suggest that you invite Mac to the dance. It'll be more fun with a date."

"I never even said I was going, Connie. You made a presumption. I remember coming down with my parents to attend when I was a teenager—it was a second chance to wear my new Easter dress—but somehow at this point in my life I can't picture myself at a church dance. As far as I'm concerned that type of function went out with spring coats."

"It's not hokey or anything," Connie insisted. "It's actually very sophisticated, and a lot of fun. A lot of people our age and younger come out for the spring social. It's one of the big events in town, and it's not limited to members of the congregation. Anyone who's willing to fork over twenty-two dollars for a ticket is welcome. And it raises money for the church, so your money goes toward a good cause."

"Oh, I don't know. Maybe I'll go, but I think it'd be best if I tried to get Uncle Teddy out of the house rather than asking Mac."

"Whattaya mean, get him out of the house? From what you tell me he goes out every day, down to the Post, volunteering at the hospital, spending weekends in Charlotte with Reggie, and fishing. I don't think I've seen him twice since the funeral." Connie hesitated. "I don't know if I should mention this to you, Monique, but there's already talk about him and Bitsy Morgan."

"Mrs. Morgan from down the street?" Monique was stunned. The sixtyish widow had been a good friend of Peggy's.

"Yes. Her husband died just before Christmas."

"I remember. She used to come over and sit with Aunt Peggy while Uncle Teddy went out. Now they have dinner together a few times a week. I have lunch or dinner with him myself two or three times every week. Because of that, people are saying they're involved? That's disgusting! My aunt's only been dead a few weeks."

Connie shrugged. "I'm just letting you know what's spreading through the grapevine. I know they've spent some time together, but I think it's because they're both a little lonely. Bitsy had no children, Reggie's over in Charlotte, and they're both alone." She placed her silverware across her now-empty plate. "If you ask me, people need to stop reading something unsavory into the friendship of two people who've both lost their spouses."

The memory of Mac's call remained at the forefront of Monique's mind all day, even though it ended quickly. He said he'd just gotten back last night from taking Jerome back home, but he wanted to say hello and ask if she'd had a nice Easter. After no contact with him for over a week, she was hoping for more—like maybe to be asked out to Chili's, after she left that gift certificate prominently propped on the center console—but at least she knew he was thinking of her. And at least he hadn't mentioned the unrestrained kiss she'd given him last Sunday evening.

But her feminine instincts told her he hadn't forgotten it any more than she had.

Chapter 18

Speculation

"Uncle Teddy, Connie was telling me about the dance the church is giving in a few weeks," Monique said as the last shot of the movie they'd rented faded. "How'd you like to escort me? I think it'll be good for you to attend a social function."

"Actually, I wanted your opinion on that, Monique. I was thinking about asking Bitsy Morgan to go with me. She spent a lot of time over here those last months Peggy was sick, since her husband died. We've had dinner together a lot of times since Peggy's funeral. She understands what I've gone through. Her husband died of cancer, too. We're just friends, but do you think people will talk?"

She used the opportunity to clear the coffee table of the drinking glasses and the large bowl containing a few unpopped kernels of popcorn to give her more time while she chose her words carefully. "People are always going to talk, Uncle Teddy, whether they need to or not. But do you really think you ought to go out on a date so soon after Aunt Peggy died?"

"But it really isn't a date, Monique. Bitsy and I are just friends, helping each other cope with our losses."

Monique remembered how she'd convinced herself that a picnic wasn't really a date, either, but that didn't stop her from kissing Mac like a woman starved, and now, twenty times a day, find herself thinking about him and how good it had felt to be in his arms. "But if you two show up together at a dance you know people are going to think otherwise," she said as she sat back down at the table. "It's not the same as having dinner together at home. Isn't that why you asked for my opinion?" she asked gently.

He looked startled. "I suppose it is. How 'bout that? How people will react has been in my subconscious all along, and I didn't even know it was there. But you know what? Let them gossip. *I* know there's nothing improper going on."

"There you go. Sometimes you just have to forget about the gossips and do what's best for you. You know I'm behind you, whatever you do."

"Thanks, Monique. I guess deep down I really am feeling a little edgy about it. But there's nothing wrong with having a friend. Bitsy and I are *not* romantically involved."

"I know. Uncle Teddy, there's something I've been meaning to talk to you about."

"What's that?"

"Well, you invited me here to run the bed-and-breakfast while Aunt Peggy was sick. Now that she's gone, I didn't know . . ."

"Say no more. You don't think I'm gonna throw you out now that Peggy's gone, do you? I know she's the one you share a bloodline with, but you and I are family regardless, Monique. I thought you knew that."

"I'm not saying I think you'll throw me out, but it's your B-and-B, and if you want to run it now that you have the time, you should be able to. I don't want you holding back because you're trying to be considerate of my feelings. I can always go back to New York."

"Well, you don't need to go rushing off anywhere until you're good and ready. It takes time to regroup after being downsized, and that can take six months, or even a year. Plus you're in the middle of remodeling. You've got plenty to do around here. Besides, I'm having a great time. I've been to Reggie's twice, and he and Gina couldn't be happier to see me. It was hard for Peggy and me to get away before because we were running the inn. In fact, when you move on I'll probably end up selling the old place."

"Really?"

"Oh, I'd probably hold on to it if I was fifteen years younger, but I'm seventy years old. I'd like to do a little traveling before it's too late."

"But you and Aunt Peggy have traveled before."

"Yeah, I know, we just hung out a shingle that said 'closed' and didn't take any bookings for the time we planned to be away, but if you want to know the truth, Monique, running the B-and-B hasn't been the same since Peggy got sick. Before that, it was something she and I did together, our little joint project. But it lost its luster for me the day the cleaning and breakfast preparation became too much for her and we had to hire Connie."

She felt her eyes growing moist. "I'm sorry, Uncle Teddy."

"It's all right. I just don't want to hear any more of this talk about you rushing back to New York. You stay as long as you want, and when you're ready to go just let me know."

Monique felt a lot better after having the talk with Teddy. When he listed the reasons she should remain in

Washington, he hadn't included her literary aspirations. Monique still wrote every day, but the process was going much slower than she anticipated it would. She knew how to spell, and she had a fairly good vocabulary. She'd thought that would make writing easy, but now she knew better. She had a lot more to learn, but she was willing to work at it, and she had. She joined a writers' group who met weekly at the library, critiquing each other's work anonymously.

Sometimes she felt overwhelmed by it all. There was so much to learn; syntax, tense, point of view, plotting, and keeping her own individual voice. She initially thought she'd have a first draft finished by now. She had been writing for nearly three months, but she only had a little over 150 pages, with probably another 250 to go. At least she felt reasonably certain that the pages she had completed were all good pages. They'd require improvements, yes, but she shouldn't have to throw anything out.

She was taking a gamble with this sabbatical, and she knew it, for employers generally didn't go for long hiatuses. The longer she stayed away, the more difficult it would be to return to the work force. Many a woman had learned that firsthand after taking time off to raise children. But Monique had worked virtually every day of her life since finishing college. There had been no extended leave for maternity, like so many women had, nor any sick leave, since she hadn't had as much as the flu in all that time. All she had were the standard weekends, holidays, and vacations. After nearly two decades of paralegal work, she found that she rather enjoyed the change of pace. Funny. She'd always enjoyed her work, but now that she wasn't doing it anymore she didn't miss it.

She was glad not to have to cope with the legendary metro Atlanta traffic. She didn't miss the runs in brand-new hosiery, or the constant trips to the dry cleaner's to drop off dirty suits and pick up clean ones. She didn't even miss the office and social gossip. She might spend more time alone in Washington, but she wasn't isolated by any means.

Teddy was right, she shouldn't be too concerned about hurrying back to work. A gut instinct kept telling her she was about to begin a new, unknown phase of her life.

She hoped it would include Mac, because now she felt ready for him.

Chapter 19

Second Chance

Connie applied perfume carefully. She wanted to smell good for Lyman, but the harsh alcohol-based product wasn't meant to be tasted. Behind the ears was okay, maybe a little dab in her cleavage, but not on her throat. She didn't want to make Lyman gag.

She felt more at ease with him than ever before. He always kissed her cheek when he showed up for work at the bed-and-breakfast, and he never failed to praise her cooking.

Lyman was so open with her, so honest. "I want to see you again, Connie," he'd said when he called her the next day. "Not just every now and then, but whenever you can." After their first date they'd quickly fallen into a routine that felt as natural as it did comfortable. Fridays he'd usually bring over some kind of takeout: pizza, Chinese, barbecued chicken or ribs. Saturdays varied. Sometimes they did the dinner-and-a-movie deal, other times they got together with his friends to view a boxing match on cable or to go to the comedy club in Greenville for a few good laughs. A couple of times they'd even stayed home and watched old commercial-free movies on the local PBS station. The one constant was that whatever they did, Connie always had a good time.

Over the past few weeks their good-night kisses had progressed from chaste to much more urgent. Just last week Lyman embraced her and whispered her name with a longing that made her forget about the extra weight she carried on her five-four frame. Knowing Lyman desired her made her feel as shapely as Halle Berry. Then and there she knew the time to bring their relationship to the next level had come. She was no longer a shy schoolgirl awed by her own sexuality, she was a middle-aged woman with a grown son.

Connie sipped her Irish coffee as she watched Lyman devour a concoction of vanilla ice cream with a drizzle of chocolate liqueur. "I never would have believed you'd be able to finish that whole thing, but it looks like you're going to."

"It's hitting the spot," he said as he swallowed. "You should try one."

"Maybe next time. It must have five hundred calories, maybe more."

He met her gaze head-on. "I noticed you've been ordering a lot of salads lately. You trying to lose weight?"

She shrugged. "I think it's a good idea, don't you?"

"I think you just asked me a loaded question. If *you* think losing weight is a good idea, then lose it. But don't do it because you think it'll make you more attractive to me. I think you're beautiful now."

The compliment caught her off guard, and in an instant her eyes filled with happy tears. To her horror she couldn't contain them. She grabbed her napkin and dabbed furiously at her eyes.

"Hey, what's wrong? What'd I say?"

"Lyman . . . you big lug," she said in a voice ringing

with affection. "I'm fine. It's just that it's been ages since anyone's told me they think I'm beautiful."

"You don't have to be 120 pounds to be considered beautiful, Connie," he said, resting his spoon in his nearly empty parfait dish. He wiped his mouth, then tossed his napkin on the table and leaned forward, taking her hand. "If only you knew how much I want you."

She felt dizzy, and her heart pounded wildly. "I think I have an idea. I felt it last Saturday when you brought me home. I felt it, too."

He applied more pressure on her hand. "When do you expect Glenn to get in?"

"Tomorrow. Early afternoon, he said, around one."

He removed several bills from his wallet and flagged down the waiter. "You're sure he's not driving in tonight?"

"Positive. He said he'd be sure to call ahead if his plans changed. I think he thinks—he might think you and I—"

"I wish we were," Lyman said wistfully. He returned the check to the waiter, along with the cash. "No change," he said to the slim young man.

"Thanks," the obviously pleased waiter said. "You folks have a good evening."

"Oh, I'm pretty sure we will," Connie said. She flashed a Cheshire Cat smile at Lyman. The haste in which he whirled her around and led her out of the restaurant told her he understood.

Connie lifted her face to Lyman. He wasn't all that tall, maybe five eleven. His bulk was what made him seem like a tree trunk of a man.

"Connie, are you sure you're ready?" he asked softly,

his fingertips gently caressing her right cheek. "If you want to change your mind, I'll understand."

She could feel the calluses on several of his fingers and knew they came from working with his hands.

"I'm sure," she said. "I just wish I was . . . as pretty as I used to be."

"C'mon, I told you not to worry about that. Here, let me show you." Lyman removed his shirt, keeping his V-neck undershirt on. He turned profile and rested both palms on his rounded belly. "Now, surely that makes you feel better."

She giggled, then began unbuttoning her yellow dotted Swiss blouse. "Well, since you're showing me yours . . ."

Chapter 19

The Way You Look Tonight

Monique broke into a cheekbone-straining smile at the approval in Mac's eyes when she opened the door for him. The rainbow tulle skirt of Peggy's dress, which had probably grazed Peggy's ankles, came to her mid-calf. Teddy had also offered her Peggy's shoes, but Monique's feet, a full size larger, couldn't fit them. She wore her own white mules.

His eyes shone, and his vocal reaction was like a symphony to her ears. "Wow!"

"I take it that means you approve."

"You look fabulous. Is that a vintage dress?"

"Absolutely. It's older than I am."

"You wear it very well."

"Thanks. I'm just about ready. Is Jerome in the car?"

"Actually, Adrian picked him up just before I left to come here, so they rode separately. They looked very sweet together."

"I'll bet."

The party was in full swing when they arrived at the restaurant banquet room a little before ten. Jerome and Adrian were dancing, her bright orange dress a bright standout in a sea of dark formal wear. Connie caught sight of them and gestured for them to join their table, where she sat with only Lyman and another couple.

Monique recognized the female of the other couple. She couldn't remember Diane Duncan's married name, but their mothers were good friends. Like herself, Diane had grown up in New York and spent summer vacations in Washington with her mother's relatives. Eventually she married a fellow from town and had lived here for over twenty years. She was about five years Monique's senior, a large enough gap that they had had little in common when they were growing up.

"Diane, how nice to see you," she greeted.

"And on a happy occasion," Diane said with a smile.

She remembered Diane paying her respects at Peggy's wake. "Yes, we knew we'd have one eventually, didn't we?"

Diane introduced her husband, Arthur Winston, and Monique presented Mac. She soon learned that Arthur and Lyman had gone through school together.

"Has anyone seen Liz?" she asked.

"Yes, I think she's in the ladies' room," Connie said.

"What about Uncle Teddy?"

"I haven't seen him yet. Liz's daughter and Mac's nephew are sitting at a table with my son and some other young people," Connie added. "You know how it is when you're in your teens and twenties. The further away from the old folks, the better." She chuckled, then turned to Diane. "Is your daughter here?"

"No, she was too busy at school to get away. But Arthur and I are going to drive up and see her tomorrow."

* * *

When the hum of voices escalated to the point where it was practically an accompaniment to the live band, Monique knew Teddy had arrived with Bitsy.

A quick glance revealed various revelers staring in their direction and poking those who hadn't noticed.

"Something seems to have caused quite a stir," Mac remarked as he scanned the room.

"It's my uncle," Monique said flatly. "He's escorting a neighbor who lost her husband recently. They've had dinner together a few times to help each other cope, but the good people of the congregation seem to be reading something sordid into their friendship. The way everyone's gawking at them I'm surprised the plucking band didn't stop playing."

Mac nodded. "I guess someone needs to remind them of the eleventh commandment, the one that goes, 'Thou shalt not gossip.'"

"It's a terrible thing, talking out of turn," Diane said. "I'll never forget when I was pregnant with Sabrina. I went up to New York to spend a week with my parents. They were excited about having their first grandchild, and I wanted to see them while I was pregnant, and let them see me. Well, don't you know it was all over town that I'd left Arthur? I felt so hurt."

"That's right," Arthur agreed cheerfully, clearly able to joke about the untrue scuttlebutt with the passage of time. "The rumor had it that I was beating her like a drum."

Monique pushed her chair back. "I think I'd better go and say hello and let people know my uncle has my support."

"I'll go with you," Mac said, quickly rising.

His arm brushed hers as they walked, and the next thing she knew he had taken her hand and laced his fingers with hers. She looked at him questioningly, and he said in a tone for her ears only, "I can tell you're tensing up, and I want you to relax and have a good time. Remember, it's a party."

She smiled, feeling her tension melt away. The feel of his hand on hers was like salve to a cut, soothing and comforting.

They returned to the table after spending a few minutes with Teddy and Bitsy. Mac and Lyman began talking about an upcoming heavyweight title bout. Diane and Arthur were dancing, and Connie was dancing with a tall, slim young man Monique knew had to be Glenn, her son. Connie brought him over after their dance, and with pride a blind person could see introduced him to Monique and Mac. The young man uttered pleasant greetings and joked briefly with Lyman before excusing himself.

"Time for a refill," Lyman said.

"Wait, I'll go with you," Mac said. "What can I get you, Monique?"

"Vodka and cranberry juice, please."

After the men left, Monique took advantage of being alone at the table to have a private conversation with Connie. She moved to the other side of the circular table to sit next to Connie, which also gave her a view of the other side of the ballroom, where Teddy and Bitsy were sitting.

Connie looked luminous in sea-green silk. "You look different somehow," Monique said. "Did you do something to your hair?"

Connie patted her short, dark tresses. "No, just a wash and set."

"Did you win the Pillsbury Bake-Off for your pancake recipe?"

"No, silly."

Monique deliberately lowered her voice so that only Connie could hear. "Did you have sex last night?"

Connie covered her mouth with tented hands, trying to hold back joyous laughter.

"I knew there was something different," Monique said triumphantly. "See, it's just like riding a bi— No, in your case I'll say like whipping up a batch of pancakes from scratch, isn't it? You never forget how to do it."

Connie shook with laughter and jabbed Monique's elbow. "You need to stop, girl!"

"All right, I'll be good." Monique scanned the room. "I want to get a glimpse at Uncle Teddy and make sure he's okay."

"Sure he is. He's sitting with his closest friends, so there's no problems at that table. The problem is with the people at the *other* tables," Connie said bitterly.

Monique felt her upper body tense. "I can tell you know something. You've got to tell me what you heard."

Connie's eyes flashed dark with anger. "People are saying Reggie's not here this year because he doesn't approve of Teddy's involvement with Bitsy"—she imitated the indignant tones of the gossipmongers— "'before his mother's cold in her grave.'"

"But that's ridiculous. Reggie's not here because he and Gina didn't have a baby-sitter. Gina's parents are the logical ones to care for their little boy, but they're here. Last year they came with Uncle Teddy, and Aunt Peggy stayed at home with the baby. She told me she just didn't feel up to going shopping for a new dress, and that she looked forward to having some time alone to bond with her grandchild. Even then she knew . . . she knew her time on earth was limited."

"I remember Teddy telling me she wanted to stay

home. But sometimes people just have to have something to talk about," Connie said. "I'm so tired of my neighbors smiling at me like they're in on some big secret. I know it has something to do with Lyman. I can only imagine what they're saying."

"I swear, if I hear anybody saying—"

Connie waved her silent. "Let it go, Monique. It's just as wrong to go looking for trouble as it is to create it."

At eleven forty-five, just fifteen minutes before the midnight breakfast was due to be served, Monique noticed Adrian emerge from the ladies' room wearing a wan expression, her hand resting on her forehead. She walked over to her young cousin. "Is something wrong, Adrian?"

"I'm getting a headache," Adrian said, half talking, half crying. "That happens to me sometimes when I'm around loud music."

Monique slipped her arm through Adrian's. "Come on, let's go see your mother. She'll want to get you home right away so you can rest."

"I can take her home," Jerome said.

Monique merely smiled at him. "You guys just come with me."

Liz had spent most of her time with a new man named Eddie who was at the dance with friends. By now she had moved to his table and was so busy conversing that she didn't notice them approaching. Monique left Adrian standing with Jerome, who put a protective arm around her shoulders, and slipped into an empty chair on Liz's right. "Liz, Adrian's not feeling well."

"Oh, no." She immediately looked at Adrian but didn't get up. "What's wrong, honey?"

"My head hurts."

"I think she should go home, Mrs. Barkley," Jerome said quickly. "I'd be happy to see that she gets there safely."

"That's awfully nice of you, Jerome. She needs to take a couple of Extra Strength Tylenol and sit in a quiet, dim room, and I'm sure she'll feel better."

Monique was stunned. Wasn't Liz going to tend to her daughter? Did meeting a new man mean so much to her that she would leave Adrian's welfare to Jerome, a teenager himself?

"C'mon, Liz, let's dance," Eddie said.

Liz got up, hugged Adrian, and instinctively felt her forehead. "No fever. You'll be fine, honey. I'll call to check on you in about half an hour." To Jerome she said, "Be sure to take her right home. She'll be all right. I'll be home in another two hours anyway."

"All right, Mrs. Barkley."

Liz and Eddie promptly headed for the dance floor. Jerome took Adrian's arm to escort her out. Monique was desperate to stall until Mac returned. She didn't want to be a busybody, but Mac was responsible for Jerome, so it was okay for him to get involved. "Are you coming back, Jerome?" she asked hastily.

"I don't think so. It won't be any fun without Adrian."

"He can take my car home and bring it back in the morning," Adrian said weakly.

"No fun? There are plenty of young people here," Monique said. "I know you're worried about Adrian, Jerome, but she'll be fine in the morning. Her mother said so." She looked around frantically. Where was Mac? He wouldn't like this any more than she did. She had a bad feeling about the whole thing. Adrian had blamed the music, but it wasn't even all that loud. "Maybe I should get Mac—" she began.

"I think he's in the men's room," Jerome said. "I really think I'd better get Adrian home as soon as possible. Good night, Monique."

"Good night." She looked after them, feeling as helpless as she felt worried.

Chapter 21

Good Night, Ladies

Monique's fingers alternated between fiddling with her beaded purse and the triple-strand fake pearls she'd bought at Wal-Mart. After exchanging numerous lingering good-nights with other partygoers in the parking lot, they were finally on their way home, and now that their own good-nights were nearly upon them, she found herself feeling fidgety and nervous. Would Mac expect another amorous kiss like the one they'd shared after the picnic? And would she be able to control her impulses and keep her ardor in check, or would his embrace once again make her forget herself . . . and everything else? She felt unsure that she would be able to control the excitement that raced through her whenever he touched her. When they danced she'd practically trembled in his arms before closing her eyes and forcing herself to concentrate on her steps.

Mac opened the driver-side door. He stopped to wave at someone driving by before hopping in. "That was a real nice evening, don't you think?"

"Oh, I enjoyed it tremendously. It's been years since I went to one, but it's considered Washington's social event of the season, at least for the black community," she said. "One of the other churches started having a similar function in the summer, but everyone says it's not as nice as ours. It's like going to a wedding without having to fork over a hundred and fifty dollars for a gift."

"It's too bad Jerome and Adrian had to cut their evening short. Adrian looked so lovely in that orange dress."

"She'll get to wear it again. Apparently the high school holds a formal dance every year, a few weeks before school lets out for the summer. Most of the lower classmen go, since the seniors have their prom. When Liz bought Adrian's dress she told her she'd have to wear it to both events."

"I guess Jerome'll be making another trip down here, if there's another dance."

"They do seem inseparable, don't they?" She frowned. "But I'm a little worried about Liz's behavior. She didn't seem all that concerned about Adrian's headache."

"You mean you expected she would bring Adrian home herself? Well, so did I. When Connie told me Jerome had taken her I asked where Liz was, and Connie said she was dancing. That about blew me away."

"Yeah, some man from Greenville who was here with some local people," Monique said. "I looked for you, Mac. I was hoping we could go along with the kids, get Adrian home safely, and then drop off Jerome, since he said he didn't want to come back without her."

"I was talking with a couple of fellows in the back. I wish I hadn't been. You know Liz better than I do, Monique. Is she the type of mother who would put her social life ahead of her daughter?"

"I'd hoped not, but I'm afraid this proves she is."

"Unsupervised teenagers can get into all types of trouble, and having been seventeen once myself, I know what *I* would've tried to do if I had the opportunity to be alone with my girlfriend," Mac said. "But it's a delicate situation. Adrian is Liz's daughter, and if Liz thinks it's okay it's really not right for you or me to intervene." He hesitated. "But I think I will have a little talk with Jerome, though."

Monique forgot all about Jerome, Adrian, and Liz when Mac pulled over in front of the B&B. Her inner voice repeatedly warned her to be cool, but each beat of her heart sounded heavy and dull, like Big Ben announcing the hour.

"I can't remember the last time I was out this late," Mac was saying.

"I understand some of the congregation wanted the dance to end at midnight," she remarked. "They were vetoed, obviously." They'd made a wise choice, in her opinion. It was after two A.M. That gave her an excuse not to invite him in.

She managed to unlock the front door without dropping her keys. She'd left a low-voltage parlor light on, as well as that of the front porch. She stepped inside, and he followed.

"You look absolutely wonderful tonight, Monique," he said, taking one last look at her ensemble. "But if I had one thing I could change, it would be to a skirt that didn't hide your legs."

She laughed. "I'll keep that in mind." She broke off, realizing she'd been about to say, "For next time," which she thought would sound rather presumptuous.

He smiled at her, and though the lighting was dim, for the first time she noticed he had a slight overbite. This certainly wasn't a particularly desirable attribute, but on him it was, well, rather cute.

"I know it's late, and I don't want to keep you up, so I'll just say good night," he said.

Her eyelids fluttered shut as he moved in closer. The first thing she felt was his fingertips gently raising her chin. When their lips made contact she experienced that same delicious feeling of weightlessness she had before. His kiss had a gentleness about it that she didn't remember . . . but perhaps her passionate display had prevented him from showing his more tender side. She was happy to let him take the lead. His fingertips caressed her jaw, and when the kiss came to its inevitable end she fervently wished they could do it again.

"It's been a long time between dates," he said softly. "Too long. I hope you don't mind if I tell you I'd like to see you again, and soon."

"I wouldn't mind at all. In fact, I look forward to it."

"Good. Talk to you soon."

"Good night, Mac."

Mac quietly let himself into his apartment. Jerome was stretched out on the opened sofa bed in the living room, dead asleep. In the room lit only by moonlight he looked maybe twelve years old. The corners of his mouth turned up slightly, like he was having a pleasant dream. The subject matter was an easy guess. Mac suspected his nephew was experiencing his first love. His sister told him Jerome had arranged to cover his coworkers' weekend shifts at the Food Lion where he stocked shelves part-time so he could get this time off. Now that summertime was approaching, Mac expected to see a lot of Jerome in Washington. And to think his nephew had met Adrian all because of a chance remark he'd made to Monique.

He liked what he'd seen tonight. Not only had Monique looked fabulous in a decades-old dress, but he found her unwavering support of her uncle touching. For a moment he'd thought her wrath for those who spoke against Teddy would dampen the evening, but she calmed down pretty quickly when he asked her to. She probably realized that being tense and angry would only give the upper hand to those who spread the rumors.

It looked like the time had come for him to admit he'd made a mistake. From what he could see, Monique Oliver was a caring, loyal woman. Maybe he'd caught her on an off day when he first checked into the B&B. Or maybe his judgment was lacking. No one could be right all the time.

He kept remembering how warm and smooth the bare skin of her back and shoulders felt when they danced. It had taken supreme willpower to keep his hands still and not roam over the surface of her mid and upper back and kiss her right there on the floor. *That* would have given the congregation plenty to gossip about.

As it was he'd better watch out, or he'd end up sleeping with that same loopy grin Jerome wore.

Chapter 22

Sweet Summer

As the warm days of spring heated up to a sizzling summer, more than just Monique's garden was in bloom. She finally completed the first draft of her manuscript and began the arduous, often frustrating task of revising and polishing. Best of all, since the dance she and Mac had fallen into an easy companionship, seeing each other fairly regularly, once or twice during the week and on weekends when he didn't go home to Raleigh. Monique was thrilled about this, but their relationship retained a casualness she found frustrating at times. For all their togetherness, she sensed an unidentifiable force keeping them apart, an invisible barrier holding Mac at a distance.

Or could it be the holdout was Mac himself?

Monique felt a pull on her line. "Mac, I think I've got a bite," she said, her voice ringing with excitement.

He was at her side in an instant. "Hold it steady. Now, reel it in slowly." He moved to stand behind her, his arm brushing against hers in his willingness to assist her.

His close proximity made Monique breathless. She fought the urge to lean against him and wrap his arms around her, forcing herself to instead concentrate on reeling in her catch. "Oh, isn't he cute?" she said when a wiggling fish with a bluish tint emerged on the end of her line. "But it doesn't look like the one you caught."

"This is a bluefish. I caught a flounder."

"Would you mind taking it off the hook for me? I like catching the fish, but I hate touching them. They're so . . . so scaly," Monique said, her mouth twisting at the thought. "Besides, one time when I was a kid I got a hook stuck in my forearm, and I don't want to relive that experience."

He chuckled. "I remember Jerome got one caught in his cheek. We had to cut the day short and get him to the emergency room."

She watched as his deft fingers removed the still-struggling fish from the hook. Mac's fingers had deep lines at the joints, and his hands had an overall rough-hewn look she would associate with someone in construction.

"Well, that's two," Mac said.

"We'll have to do better than that if all of us are going to eat tonight, Mac."

"Oh, we'll eat, all right, but somebody might have to have a hamburger," he said with a chuckle. "That's why they call it 'fishing,' not 'catching.'"

She wiped her damp forehead with a paper towel. "I don't know how much more of this heat I can stand. My sunscreen is vanishing into my skin as fast as I can apply it."

"Want to pack it in and cool off with a dip?"

"Sounds like a good idea, but let's stay out for another half hour, forty-five minutes. Maybe we'll catch some more." She reached for the plastic water bottle at her side and took a long gulp. Eastern North Carolina, always hot in the summer, was experiencing a brutal heat wave. Mac was dressed appropriately for the high mercury reading in cutoff jeans and rubber-soled black Speedo sandals, which he slipped off before dangling his feet over the side of the pier. She, too, wore shorts, and she happily caught his gaze lingering on her legs. He'd get another chance to look at them when they went swimming in an hour. Their campground was in Cape Hatteras, right on the ocean.

She'd initially been shocked when Mac asked her to go camping with him and Jerome and Jerome's younger sister, Shaun. He explained that he took his niece and nephew on long weekend camping trips two or three times a year. Monique hadn't been able to conceal her initial distaste for the idea, and she hastily explained to Mac that she'd never gone camping before, not wanting him to think she was a prima donna. "I'm afraid my idea of vacation is a full-service Marriott," she'd said, trying to make a joke of it.

It had been difficult for Monique to fathom why anyone would want to spend part of their vacation up close and personal with nature, but she couldn't deny the fun she was having. The KOA campground featured designated areas for campers to park RVs and for those who merely pitched tents, like them. She did find herself looking longingly at the simple log cabins with their conveniences like wood-frame beds and mattresses, electric lights, doors that locked—and kept out bears!—even air-conditioning. Mac, Jerome, and Shaun scoffed at them, saying the people staying in them weren't really roughing it like they were, that slumbering on a mattress inside a cabin wasn't the same as sleeping in sleeping bags in the great outdoors, with just a thin tent between them and the same expansive sky seen all over the world. But as good a time as Monique was having, she sure as heck wouldn't mind a little more comfort. The first night she'd dreamed of both snakes and grizzly bears and awakened in a cold sweat.

But overall she was enjoying this new experience. The pancakes they made for breakfast and the hamburgers at lunch, all cooked on Mac's portable grill, were the best she'd tasted, even better than Connie's. She supposed the whole outdoor factor served to sharpen her taste buds. Never had pancakes tasted so fluffy and bacon so crisp and flavorful.

Steaming-hot showers and clean facilities were just steps away, as were an abundance of activities. The camp was neatly tucked between the Atlantic Ocean on the east and two sparkling pools on the west. Jerome and Shaun were having a great time enjoying activities with the dozens of other teenagers present, like bike riding, swimming, and parasailing. Mac would have brought Adrian along as well, but she had flown to Thailand after school let out to spend a month visiting her army officer father and his second family.

Monique and Mac preferred less strenuous activities, like lounging in the hot tub or fishing from the pier. She had gone fishing in the Pamlico River as a child, when her father and Teddy would go out in a rowboat and bring her and Reggie along. But that had been a long time ago, and she never expected to ever again become ecstatic over getting a nibble from a fish. Yet here she was.

Monique liked the nights most of all. Due to the close confines of the tent, her sleeping bag was only inches away from Mac's. Last night he'd pleasantly startled her by reaching for her hand and bringing it to his lips, and when he lowered their hands to a more natural position he held on to hers, and they fell asleep that way. The action went a long way toward easing her impatience at the nearly unbearable slow progression of their relationship.

She loved to watch him while he slept. He looked so peaceful, so placid . . . at least when there were no ungracious snorts coming from his mouth. She and the kids teased him about his rather loud snores.

In spite of Monique's eagerness to have Mac as her lover, it pleased her that they had become friends. That element had been missing from her relationships with Ozzie and Skye and Gregory, as well as the other men in her life, and she felt it boded well for their future. Her only complaint remained how slow they seemed to be moving. She tried to tame her anxiousness to move to the next level, but she'd love to have that look of happy contentment, like the one Connie wore since she and Lyman had taken that step.

"I do admit I'm feeling pretty happy these days," Connie said one morning over breakfast in response to Monique's telling her how good she looked. "I never thought I'd feel this way about anyone again after Charles died. And I don't mind telling you I was very worried about how Glenn was going to react. But he and Lyman get along real well." She met Monique's skeptical glance with a knowing smile. "Don't get me wrong. I know there'll come a time eventually when they'll have a disagreement over something or other, but what they're doing now is laying a good foundation. Glenn even asked Lyman for his opinion about how to approach some girl he likes at school. He waited until I left the room to bring it up, but Lyman told me about it after. And Glenn told me he's glad I have someone in my life."

"You should be very proud that you raised a son who's so concerned about your happiness, Connie. A lot of kids today only care about themselves."

"Oh, I think a lot of that has to do with how they're raised. Take Diane Winston's daughter, Sabrina. That girl never even wants to come home."

Monique frowned. Could Connie be speaking out of turn? How much did she really know about Sabrina Winston? "Why do you say that, just because she didn't make it to the dance? Doesn't that seem a little unfair?"

"No, I'm saying that because she never comes home," Connie said flatly. "She only gets here occasionally, like last Christmas. I think she spent Thanksgiving with the family of one of her school friends. And she's not home now, even though it's summer break. She took a job as a camp counselor somewhere way up in the Pocono Mountains of Pennsylvania."

"That does seem odd," Monique said. "Not a lot of pay, and away from home all summer to boot. What do you suppose the problem is?"

"I *know* what the problem is. The poor girl's being smothered." Connie shook her head sympathetically. "Diane and Arthur won't let up. They drive to Raleigh literally every weekend to see her. No college kid wants to see their parents every single week."

"If they were going to do all that, maybe she should have stayed in Washington and commuted to a local college," Monique mused. "That way Diane and Arthur wouldn't have to drive so far every weekend."

Connie shook her head. "The point isn't how far they drive each week, Monique. Glenn says the kids at school tease Sabrina about being her parents' little baby. Diane and Arthur never learned to let go, and I think it's going to come back and haunt them. Sabrina's already nineteen, and by the time she graduates from college she's not going to want to be bothered with them at all. I hope she doesn't move to some faraway city and shut them out of her life completely." She paused. "I think Glenn kind of likes her. He sounded so disappointed when he told me about her plans to be a camp counselor."

"He'll see her again when the fall semester starts," Monique said as she enjoyed the last bite of her omelet. "By the way, Connie, how often do you go to see Glenn?"

"Never. I did go with him this year and last when he got set up, to make sure everything was okay. Actually, I drove behind him. We needed two cars to carry all his stuff, his TV, stereo, computer, clothes. I met his roommate and his roommate's parents. Nice people, from Delaware, I think. I saw the room they're staying in, which lets me picture his surroundings when we talk on the phone. Now that he'll be a junior I probably won't even go with him to set up. I feel college is his personal territory, and I don't want to intrude."

"Well, since he comes home every couple of weeks, I'd say you're doing the right thing." The conversation made Monique recall what Liz had said that day at the mall in Greenville. "It's a good thing you never had kids, Monique. They'd never be able to breathe." She couldn't help wondering if she, like Diane and Arthur Winston, would have been an overbearing parent.

But Liz was as dissatisfied with the status quo as Connie was happy. "You never want to go out anymore, Monique," she complained one Friday over a casual, somewhat sloppy lunch at BW-3 Wings.

"That's not true. You and I went to a club just last week."

"And you left early. I'll never meet my Mr. Right sitting home in Washington. You're just not any fun since you started dating Mac."

Monique loudly bit into a celery stick, clearly getting a kick out of the crunching noise it made. "That's not true, Liz. I wasn't much fun, as you put it, even *before* that. But you and I have different definitions of fun. I've tried to get you to go bowling or to play golf. But all you want to do is go to clubs, and I'm not into the party scene anymore. I don't like being around all that smoke. It makes me want to light up myself, and I'm trying to quit. So because you're not interested I do those things with Connie." She discreetly removed a chicken particle lodged between her back teeth with a toothpick.

"I probably wouldn't be into it either, if I had somebody I could stay home with. Some people have all the luck. You've got Mac, Connie's got Lyman . . . even Adrian's got Jerome. Those two are tighter than last year's jeans."

"First love," Monique said with a smile.

"Adrian carried on like it was the end of the world when I told her I didn't feel she should go to Jerome's graduation," Liz continued. "His mother called me and assured me Adrian would be properly chaperoned in her home and would room with her daughter, but I felt it was too much. Adrian won't even be seventeen until August."

"For whatever it's worth, I agree with you, Liz. She's a little young yet to be attending her boyfriend's out-of-town high school graduation." Mac had expressed the same sentiment, but Monique didn't want to mention his name in their conversation, not after Liz pointed out that everyone was seeing someone except her. No need to emphasize it.

"I figured Jerome would be getting on a Greyhound every two or three weeks to spend the weekends here," Liz said. "The last thing I expected was for him to come to spend the summer with Mac and get a job here. Adrian won't even be back from Thailand for another two weeks. He's already offered to go with me to the airport when I go pick her up." She sighed heavily. "Why is it I'm the only one who's alone? I try harder than any of you, but I keep meeting these jokers, like Cornel from the spa and Eddie from the dance. Players, both of them, just out for what they can get."

Monique tried to choose her words carefully. "Maybe you try too hard, Liz. Take a break. Sometimes love strikes when you least expect it."

"Love? Are you and Mac in love?"

Monique realized too late what she'd said. Doggone it, her plucking subconscious had sneaked its way to the forefront of her mind. "No. What Mac and I are doing is getting to know each other. I'm speaking in general terms, not about me specifically." It wasn't a complete lie, for she and Mac were doing just that. The subliminal thought she inadvertently expressed meant she had to work harder on controlling the impatient part of her nature that always wanted to rush. She wanted Mac so badly she physically ached. It was as if she had an itch that only his touch could relieve. But it was hard to be romantic with Jerome around, and with Adrian off in Thailand he was around often. When Jerome wasn't with them Mac usually wanted to get home quickly because he didn't want to leave him alone too long.

She told herself the delay was worth it. There would be no more fiascos like what she'd had with Skye. The next time it would be from-the-heart genuine, from her heart to his, and hopefully right back again. She felt that all her soul-searching would pay off with happiness like she'd never known. And it really hadn't even been that hard. She might have to check herself every now and then when she caught herself having a self-centered thought, but she'd come a long way from the woman she used to be, and she felt proud of her efforts. Selfishness had been replaced by compassion, impatience with understanding, and self-indulgence with shopping at discount stores like Wal-Mart.

"But if you do want to look at me specifically," Monique continued, "remember that I wasn't interested in meeting anyone when I moved to Washington. I was determined not to make a mess of my next relationship. And boom! Mac checks in to the B-and-B. He literally showed up on my doorstep."

"I'm happy for you, Monique, really I am, but I feel left out. I'm forty years old, just like you. It's been nearly ten years since Jerry and I were divorced. He was remarried within three or four years and has two more children. Adrian will be leaving for college in another year. She's already decided she wants to go to my alma mater, Elizabeth City State. Sometimes I think I'm going to be spending the rest of my life alone."

Liz looked so forlorn, and Monique's heart went out to her. It hadn't been that long ago that she'd felt that way herself, when in short order she'd lost Gregory, her job, and her hair. She remembered a long-ago summer when they were maybe nine or ten years old and laying out their life's plans as they passed time on a rainy afternoon. "I want to get married and have four kids, two boys and two girls," Liz had said. "My husband will be handsome and make a lot of money, and we'll live in a big house and go to parties and give parties and everything will be perfect." Liz's dream didn't include a divorce and the emotional strain of raising a daughter virtually alone. But of course most adults knew the dreams of youth often didn't come true. It certainly hadn't been *her* dream to be forty and single.

"I wish I knew the answer, Liz," Monique said slowly. "Maybe the problem is that you're always hoping to meet Mr. Right. That's why I'm suggesting you take a break, like I did. Another thing about that. I've never had so many men flirt with me in my life than I have since the day I vowed not to date again until I had it together. It started the day I arrived, and it hasn't stopped yet. Even Lyman used to flirt with me until he took a good look at Connie. A trip to the barbershop to get my hair trimmed is agony, since it's full of men hitting on me."

"See what I mean? Why can't I have that kind of luck?" Liz snapped her fingers. "I know. I'll cut my hair, so I can go to the barber, too!"

Monique knew Liz was only kidding, but nonetheless she quickly averted her eyes downward, not wanting Liz to see the pitying expression they held.

Chapter 23

It's Gotta Be Somebody's Fault

Monique answered the phone expectantly, but her good mood vanished with Mac's first words.

"I know we were supposed to have dinner tonight, Monique, but I'm afraid I'm going to have to cancel."

Her back straightened with tension. "Is something wrong?"

"Something urgent's come up. I'll fill you in on it tomorrow."

Her first instinct was to try to coax him into telling her what was wrong now—to heck with waiting—but she knew he meant what he said, and cajoling from her would only annoy him. The old Monique would behave that way, not the new and improved version. Her curiosity would have to wait to be satisfied, and that was that.

"All right," she finally said. "But you can call me later if you want to talk. I'll be up late."

Mac and Jerome wiped their feet before entering Liz's house and taking seats in the living room. Liz and Mac sat on the sofa with a space between them. Jerome sat on the love seat. Adrian wasn't in the room.

Liz cleared her throat. "I'll get right to the point," she said. "I think Adrian's pregnant."

"Pregnant?" Mac repeated incredulously. He stared at Jerome, who had sat up straight, suddenly wide-eyed. "Jerome, I asked if you knew why Mrs. Barkley wanted to see us this evening, and you said you didn't."

"I wasn't lying, Uncle Mac. I didn't know anything about it."

"Let's not fool with semantics, Jerome," Mac snapped. "You obviously knew there was a *possibility* of this happening. Even after we talked about how important it is to prevent it."

Jerome averted his eyes, not answering. Liz shot a stricken look at Mac. "You mean you *knew* they were—"

"No, Liz, I didn't know," he said gently. "But I know how kids feel and how they are. I wouldn't be fulfilling my responsibility to Jerome if I didn't address the subject."

"I caught Adrian throwing up in the bathroom this morning," Liz said. "I asked her if she'd eaten anything unusual or anything that didn't taste right. The guilty look in her eyes told me it didn't have anything to do with food. That's when I called you."

"Is she here now?" Jerome asked.

"She's upstairs. I told her to stay there."

"Maybe you should ask her to come down," Mac suggested. "The four of us need to talk about this."

"All right, if you think that's best." Liz glared at Jerome as she passed him on her way to the foot of the stairs.

Adrian went straight to Jerome's arms when she came into the room.

"If you two can pull yourselves apart," Mac said pointedly, "we've got a problem to address."

Liz had sat on the love seat when she returned to the

room, and the teens had no choice but to sit apart, Adrian with her mother and Jerome in a chair.

Mac leaned forward, his mouth and chin hidden by tented hands with intertwined fingers. Then he leaned back a little, his hands dropping to rest palms down on either side of him with his elbows bent. "I think I speak for Liz as well as myself when I say I can't tell you how disappointed I am," he finally said. "You say you don't want to be treated like babies, but you've behaved very irresponsibly. Sixteen and seventeen is old enough to know how your lives will change by starting a family. What about college?"

"I'll be seventeen in a few weeks," Adrian said. "And Jerome will be eighteen in September."

"I can still go to college, Uncle Mac," Jerome said.

"You can? And how's the child going to eat?"

"I'll set up my schedule so that I can work full-time. The supermarket manager in Raleigh was talking about putting me in their youth management program when I turn eighteen, so I'll be making more money."

"You work at the Food Lion, Jerome. 'More money' means maybe fifty cents an hour," Mac scoffed.

"I'll be able to go to college too, Mom," Adrian said. "I'll go to night school so I can work during the day."

"And who's going to take care of the baby while you're busy with school and work?" Liz asked coldly. When Adrian merely looked at her with wide eyes, Liz said, "I thought so. I'm supposed to give up all my social plans so I can change dirty diapers and quiet a screaming infant."

"At least it'll keep you at home," Adrian shot back.

No, she didn't, Mac thought, raising an eyebrow.

Liz leaned away from her daughter and raised her chin defiantly. "And what's that supposed to mean, young lady?"

"It means you won't be out chasing after some man."

Mac saw the slap coming before Adrian did. The girl gasped and rubbed the side of her face with her palm. "Sit down," he ordered Jerome, who quickly rose out of his chair to go to Adrian's aid.

"You don't tell me what I should or shouldn't be doing, little girl," Liz said sternly to Adrian. "I'm your mother, in case you forgot. Besides, last time I looked you were the only child living here. You're not crowded by a houseful of brothers and sisters that I started pumping out when I was seventeen. I didn't even have *you* until I was a responsible married woman who had finished college." She leaned against the chair back, obviously satisfied that she'd made her point.

Mac spoke again. "Adrian, has your condition been confirmed?"

"No. I was too afraid to do anything. I didn't even tell Jerome."

He felt relieved to learn Jerome had no prior knowledge of the situation, although his disappointment at his nephew's carelessness lingered like onions on a hamburger. "Well, I think we need to do that before we do anything else. Once we know for sure we can go from there." He looked questioningly at Liz, silently inquiring if she had anything to add.

"Yes, I'll bring her to a doctor next week. In Greenville," she added.

"I guess that's it, then. Unless you have something else, Liz, we'll be on our way."

"Uncle Mac," Jerome began. "Is it okay if I talk to Adrian for a couple of minutes?"

He'd been expecting this request and had his answer ready. "Not now. Right now you've got an appointment to talk to *me*. Good night, Liz, Adrian."

The teens reached out and clasped hands, holding on desperately for just a few seconds before Jerome's departure forced them to relinquish their hold.

"Pregnant!" Monique exclaimed. "Oh, no, Mac. This is awful."

He took a long gulp of the can of Coors she'd provided him with. "I'll say it's awful. This has the potential to change the course of both their lives. My sister will be devastated if Jerome doesn't go to college this fall. She's done everything for those kids, and for her it hasn't been easy. She suffers from lupus and is sometimes in terrible pain. But I've told Jerome not to say anything to her until we know for sure."

"So Adrian hasn't been to the doctor?"

"No. She's just been throwing up in the morning," he said wryly. "Liz said she'll take her to the doctor next week." He pursed his lips and exhaled loudly. "Damn kids, jumping into bed together. They hardly know each other. And Jerome completely ignored the advice I gave him about practicing safe sex. He said they've been sleeping together every chance they've had since the night of the church dance, when Adrian conveniently got a headache."

"Conveniently? You mean she really was faking?"

"I got the truth out of Jerome. They hit on a plan early in the evening, to give them some time alone. Adrian apparently was counting on her mother being one of the people who'd stay at the dance until they literally locked the front door, even if Adrian became acutely ill."

Monique shifted uncomfortably. On several occasions she'd tried to convince Liz that they didn't have to be the last ones out at the end of the evening, but Liz always feared she might miss something. How sad that Liz's own daughter viewed her as more of a party girl than a mother. "Mac, I can't tell you how sorry I am. I almost feel a little responsible, since I was the one who suggested they meet." Once more she remembered Sarah and Peggy saying she should be a good influence on Liz. She felt as if she'd let them down, especially Peggy.

"That's ridiculous. You were sweet to offer to invite Adrian to the picnic when I said I was afraid Jerome might be bored. You thought they might hit it off, and of course they did. But that's not the same as encouraging them to sleep together." He attempted a smile and was only partially successful. "Believe me, Monique, I didn't ask to come over here tonight so I could blame you. I guess I just wanted someone to talk to, and no one's a better candidate than you. You're familiar with the situation and all the parties involved."

She'd been thrilled when he rang her doorbell, thinking he was too anxious to see her to wait until the morning, but the boost to her ego was quickly forgotten when he told her what had occurred. "Do you think Adrian might consider an abortion?"

"A sixteen-year-old in love? I don't think so," he said. "Then there's the religious factor. I don't know what her beliefs are. I know *I* don't like the idea of terminating a pregnancy myself. But the main problem here seems to be the bad feelings between her and Liz. I got the distinct impression that Adrian feels a little neglected while Liz, as she put it, is out 'chasing men.' My guess is that she'll view a baby as someone who'll always be there to love her."

Monique inhaled sharply. "Adrian accused Liz of chasing men?"

"She did, but Liz put her in her place. Her cheek is probably still stinging. I think she'll watch what she says from now on." He chuckled. "If Adrian tests positive I guess I'll mention terminating the pregnancy and see how she reacts. But this whole thing makes me very uneasy, Monique. If the two of them didn't have the sense to use birth control in the past, what's to stop them from doing it in the future? Even if Adrian consents to an abortion, I certainly don't want them using it as a means of birth control." He shrugged. "Then again, maybe I shouldn't even worry about it. I've got a feeling that Liz plans to do everything she can to keep those two apart."

"Is there anything I can do, Mac?"

He pulled her forward and kissed her lips lightly. "You've made me feel a lot better already, and for that I thank you."

Monique slept badly. In spite of Mac's assurances, she still felt a certain amount of responsibility for the trouble Adrian and Jerome had gotten into. Even if they were sleeping together—and in their unsupervised environment they'd certainly had numerous opportunities to do so—she'd been so sure they'd use protection. The fact that they hadn't alarmed her as much as it had Mac.

She called Liz the next morning. "Hi, it's Monique. I saw Mac last night, and he told me what's happening. I just called to see if there's anything I can do."

Liz sighed heavily. "No, Monique. I think you've done enough already."

Monique's spine stiffened. "What's that supposed to mean?"

"It means that if you'd minded your business and not offered to introduce my daughter to that horny Jerome, somebody else's daughter would be pregnant right now."

"Liz, that's not fair and you know it."

"All I know is that my daughter's once-bright future is now a huge question mark. She was going to go to college next year. Motherhood at seventeen just isn't part of the plan, and neither is me raising another baby at forty. I resent that this is what we're faced with just because you wanted to get in good with Mac. So now you and Mac are nice and cozy, and I'm preparing to be a grandmother."

"I'm very sorry you feel that way," Monique said stiffly. "Like I said, I called to see if there was anything I could do to help."

"And like I said, you've helped enough already."

Monique's eyes narrowed. She wasn't about to allow herself to be the target of Liz's frustration. The best thing she could do was get off the phone right now before the conversation turned even uglier. "Good-bye, Liz," she said, and hung up. After a day or two Liz would realize how horrible she sounded and would call to apologize.

But the days went by with no word. Monique didn't tell anyone about Liz's hurtful words, not Teddy, not Connie, and not Mac. Once they patched things up it wouldn't be necessary for anyone to even know they'd ever been on the outs.

Mac called on Wednesday. "Good news. Adrian's pregnancy test was negative."

She let out a relieved sigh and said a silent prayer of thanks. "That's wonderful, Mac. I was hoping that whatever symptoms she was experiencing had something to do with that long flight back from Thailand. It was halfway around the world, after all. And of course, we can do things to ourselves just by being nervous."

"That's what her doctor said. But Liz and I decided the best thing now is for Jerome to go back to Raleigh.

It's practically impossible for her to keep tabs on Adrian while she's at work, and of course I'm working myself."

"How did Jerome take that news?"

"He's very disappointed, but he should have thought about that before he acted so irresponsibly. I'm not working Saturday, so I'll drive him back early that morning and come back Sunday." He paused for a few seconds. "Would you like to come along?"

"I'd love to," she answered without hesitation. "I'm sure Uncle Teddy won't mind taking care of the B-and-B. He did it when we went camping. I'll just check with him to make sure he doesn't have any plans for this weekend. He goes to Reggie's fairly regularly now."

She was grinning in anticipation when she hung up. A weekend in Raleigh with Mac. She'd get to see his house, perhaps even sleep in his bed. She was sure his house had at least two bedrooms, but a lot of people were setting up home offices in spare bedrooms these days. Mac, being a true gentleman, would insist she sleep where it was most comfortable.

She felt closer to him than she ever had before. Over the past weeks they'd become friends who genuinely enjoyed each other's company, friends who shared their troubles. It was, as Connie had said, a good foundation for a strong relationship.

Only one cloud blocked the sunny forecast, and it was time she did something about it. Monique picked up the receiver and dialed Liz's number. "I heard the good news," she said simply on hearing her cousin's familiar voice. "I just wanted to say how glad I am it all worked out." She waited expectantly. Surely Liz would apologize for her cruel words on Saturday.

"Yes, everything's just dandy," Liz said caustically. "My daughter's sulking at me because I suggested her teenage lover leave town. I just have to get her through the next couple of days before he leaves so there's no opportunity for her to get knocked up for real. But I guess you wouldn't know anything about that, being you don't have any kids."

Monique felt her patience evaporate like a puddle in the summer sun. "You want to tell me what's going on here, Liz? Why are you so hostile?"

"I already told you that, Monique."

"The last time we talked I figured you lashed out at me because I happened to be available, but I can't believe that after all this time you still feel I'm responsible. Sure, when Mac said he wished he knew someone Jerome's age I thought of Adrian. That's not a crime." Her annoyance grew with each word. "Maybe if you concentrated more on worrying about your daughter's welfare and less about having a good time, you wouldn't be in this predicament now."

"Don't give me that. I'm not stupid, Monique. I know Mac told you all about what Adrian said to me Friday night, and now you want to use it against me."

"Mac didn't tell me anything. I'll never forget how disappointed I was in you when you allowed Jerome to bring Adrian home when she had that headache, because you were too busy dancing with some low-life player from Greenville." Monique bit her lip, determined not to say anything more. She'd already said too much. She'd already denied Mac confiding in her about Adrian's disrespectful, if not entirely untrue, remark to her mother; and to further preserve his confidence she simply couldn't say that she knew the relationship between Jerome and Adrian had turned sexual the night of the dance, even if she'd suspected all along that Adrian was faking. "Think about it, Liz. And call if you need me. We're family, in case you've forgotten." She hung up.

Chapter 24

Satisfaction

The sting of Liz's words remained even as Monique prepared for her weekend in Raleigh, but she was determined not to let her cousin's hostile attitude spoil her weekend. Teddy had agreed to be on call for the guests and make breakfast. "You're still young, Monique," he said. "You *should* be going away for the weekend and having fun. Don't worry, I'll take care of everything."

Most summer weekends saw at least two of the four guest rooms occupied for reserved stays, and a third room frequently utilized for drop-ins. Monique had increased the rates slightly after the remodeling, and the newly furbished rooms were a hit with the guests.

Mac and Jerome came to pick her up at eight o'clock Saturday morning. "I haven't been able to spend the better part of a weekend at home since Easter," Mac remarked. "We're finally back on schedule, so it doesn't look like I'll be working on Saturdays like I used to unless we get a lot of rain and fall behind again."

"I know that makes you happy," Monique said. She glanced in the backseat. One look at the sullen Jerome and she knew he wouldn't be contributing to the conversation. "How are home sales going, anyway?"

"A little sluggish right now. We were going gangbusters in the winter and spring. Those homes are either completed or about three-quarters done. Everyone wants to close and move in before school starts. We're putting up a couple of spec homes now on the smaller lots. In a year it'll all be finished."

The corners of Monique's mouth turned upward. Mac would be in Washington for at least another year. What a nice, comfortable length of time.

Just before ten A.M. Mac pulled up to a cozy-looking white-frame house with green trim and a wide front porch. Monique was happy to have reached their destination after a ride filled with tension. She didn't feel right laughing and talking with Mac when she knew Jerome was feeling so miserable in the backseat. She didn't remember love being so painful at that age, but perhaps Jerome's feelings ran deeper than those of a typical seventeen-year-old. That probably made a lot of sense, for he'd already lost his father, grandfather, and most recently his grandmother; and his mother suffered from a painful medical condition that probably wouldn't be fatal but definitely complicated her life.

"I'll get your bags," Mac offered. Jerome ran to the front door and unlocked it with a key.

Monique took the smaller of Jerome's two bags and followed Mac up the porch stairs and into the house. Mac put the suitcase down near the foot of the stairs, and she placed the matching tote on top of it.

"Hello there," Mac said, spreading his arms wide. The tiny woman opposite him practically disappeared in the embrace.

Shaun put down the dust cloth she held and rushed to greet Monique. Monique and Mac's niece had become good friends during the camping trip to Cape Hatteras.

"This is Monique, Mom," Shaun said.

"Hello, Monique. I'm Donna. I've heard a lot about you, from both my children and my brother, and I'm glad to finally meet you."

"Hi, Donna. Mac has told me about you, too."

"Please sit down."

"Just for a minute, though, Donna," Mac said. "I'm kind of anxious to get home."

"Cora might be there, cleaning up. She said she was going to give it a good dusting before you got here. We weren't expecting you this early. Didn't you have to work today?"

"No. I think my Saturdays will be free for a while, so you'll probably see a lot of me on the weekends."

An excited chill ran through Monique's upper body like a lightning bolt. Perhaps his inviting her along this weekend, which she interpreted as a casual, spur-of-the-moment suggestion, had more depth to it than she realized. She hadn't known he was planning on spending subsequent weekends at his home here, but he had. Could it be he intended for her to make at least some of those trips with him? Taking weekend trips together suggested some kind of commitment to each other, a sign that they would soon be more than just friends, at least if all went well. As the Emergency Broadcast System said in those annoying commercials, this was a test.

And she was determined to pass it.

"Isn't that funny?" Donna was saying. "Your work-load is slowing down, and mine's heating up. I worked till six-thirty last night. We've got a huge mailing to get out."

"Do you work full-time, Donna?" Monique asked, careful to keep the surprise out of her voice. Somehow she'd expected Mac's sister to be on disability. She didn't have the look of a healthy person. Her thinness was so pronounced that her facial features seemed unusually large.

"Yes." She named a major insurance company. "I'm in the public relations department. Fortunately, they're able to accommodate me when my illness precludes me from going in. Oh, I'm sorry; I'm not thinking. Are you guys hungry?"

"No, we had breakfast before we left."

"I did too, but I'm gonna get somethin' else," Jerome said. He disappeared, presumably into the kitchen, Shaun tagging behind him, playfully warning him not to make a mess after she'd just cleaned up.

Donna looked after her son with concerned eyes. She turned to Mac the moment he was gone. "Is he all right?"

"He's mad at the world right now, but I'm sure he'll get over it and realize he only has himself to blame," Mac said. "He'll probably tell you about it once we're gone. I think this is a good time for us to cut out."

They said their good-byes, calling out to Jerome and Shaun, and Mac hugged his sister once more.

"You're very close, aren't you?" Monique asked a little enviously when they were back in the Explorer. She would have loved to have siblings, especially a sister.

"Donna is only a year younger than me, followed by Cora, who we might find tidying up my house when we get there. But all seven of us are close, especially now that it's just us. You'll meet a lot of my family this weekend."

Monique soon learned Mac wasn't kidding. Before

the day was over they'd stopped to see his youngest sister, her husband, and their new baby, just ten days old, as well as gone to visit his eight-year-old nephew, who was in the hospital recovering from a hernia operation. While there she met the boy's parents.

They had just returned from dinner when they encountered Paul, another of Mac's brothers and the second oldest male in the family. She scowled when Mac began honking frantically to catch Paul's attention before he gave up and drove off, knowing that in the darkness of the car Mac wouldn't notice. She'd been looking forward to a nice, quiet evening with just the two of them, especially after being on the go and being around so many people all day.

Paul promptly turned off his engine and got out of the car. After the brothers exchanged a big bear hug and Paul politely shook Monique's hand, he went with them into the house.

As he and Mac caught up, Monique mentally counted off all the people she'd met today. First there was Mac's sister Donna when they dropped off Jerome, then Cora when they arrived at Mac's, who'd been straightening up just as Donna predicted. Then it was off to see his sister Leslie and her baby. At the hospital she met his brother Michael, and now Paul. Five of six siblings in eight hours. Talk about a homecoming weekend. She didn't know about Mac, but she could do with less family togetherness. A whole lot less.

She forced herself to look interested when the conversation inevitably turned to Jerome and why he had cut his summer in Washington so short. She'd heard it discussed earlier today, and more than once. Goodness, the entire family was being filled in on Adrian's pregnancy scare. They reminded Monique of the family portrayed on Showtime's *Soul Food*, where everyone was into everyone else's business. In her opinion they'd have no problem if they'd cut out all the meddling, but perhaps that was the norm for large families. If the Mc-Donalds lived in Washington, the news would be all over town and Liz would be mortified. But here in Raleigh Adrian was a nameless, faceless girlfriend of Jerome's, so it really didn't matter.

Paul stayed until nearly ten o'clock. By then Monique could barely conceal how tired she was. She'd stifled a dozen yawns. When they first arrived Mac had taken her through his home and shown her the guest room with a double bed where she'd be sleeping, but she didn't feel it was right to retire without talking with Mac privately first, reviewing the day, and making sure all was well.

"Wow, it's almost ten," Mac said when he closed the door behind Paul. "Where'd the time go?"

She tried to answer, but instead another yawn escaped from her mouth, one she couldn't cover up. "Excuse me."

"You must be beat," he said as he sat beside her on the sofa. "It's been a long day. You can go in whenever you want."

"Aren't you tired, Mac? It's been just as long a day for you, and on top of that you did the driving."

He shrugged. "Under normal conditions I'd probably be unconscious with sleep, but this thing with Jerome really has me upset. I've preached safe sex to him since he was thirteen years old. Pregnancy is only one possible consequence of not using condoms. He's too old to have the attitude that 'it can't happen to me.'"

"I think most young people feel that way. Everything bad happens to other kids, not to them."

"Unfortunately, I can't worry about most young people, but I am concerned about Jerome. He's going to have to learn to control his urges. At the time of the dance they really didn't even know each other that well. In this day and age there's too much at stake to indulge in casual sex, just hopping into bed with someone because they look good to you. He was thinking with the wrong damn head."

He took another slug of beer, and she wondered if there was another reason for his being so agitated. For all she knew he felt as sexually frustrated as she did. Maybe it was time she just asked him straight out.

The thought made all traces of fatigue leave her body. Monique put down her wineglass and turned her body to face him. "Mac, do you want to make love to me?"

He looked startled by her boldness, but quickly recovered. "I guess it shows, huh? As upset as I am with Jerome, I'm also a little bit jealous, wanting you like I have for so long." He broke into a wide grin as he stood before her and extended his hand. "Was that an invitation? Because if it wasn't I'm afraid I'm about to be humiliated."

She smiled. "Can I presume that since you're so angry with Jerome for not using protection, you're never without it?"

"It's not like I've got a year's supply in my nightstand, but I'm prepared, yes."

She took his hand and in an instant was in his arms. Their kiss this time was reminiscent of the very first one they'd shared, wild and passionate, their heads moving from side to side, their tongues mingling hungrily, with the addition of his hands roving over her body, lifting and squeezing her rear, covering her breasts through the thin fabric of her sleeveless blouse. Then in a sudden motion that made her slip-on shoes fall from her feet, he lifted her and carried her to the master bedroom, his hand sturdy and reassuring around the back of her thighs.

He laid her on the bed and stretched out on top of her, leaving enough space to unbutton her blouse as he kissed her again and again. Her bra hooked in the front, and he nuzzled and nibbled at her breasts. Monique relinquished her arms from around his neck and lay with her eyes closed, her palm gently cradling the back of his head.

"Take a shower with me," he said suddenly.

She wasn't sure she could stand a delay, but she understood his reasons and couldn't dispute them. They'd been active all day, in the heat of summer. Besides, a brisk shower was sure to keep fatigue from suddenly returning. How awful it would be if she were to yawn in the middle of a passionate moment. She nodded agreement.

"I'll get it started," he said, kissing her briefly. "Come in when you're ready. But don't take too long."

He disappeared into the adjoining bathroom, and soon she heard the sound of a shower spray. She quickly removed the rest of her clothing and went to join him, merely pulling back the curtain and stepping in. He was vigorously soaping his chest, but stopped to openly assess her naked form. She took the same opportunity to perform a not-so-quick scan of his. They laughed when each realized what the other was doing, and he took her in his arms and turned her around so she stood directly under the spray. Water poured over them as they kissed. She'd never experienced such an erotic sensation. It was like kissing in a violent rainstorm.

* * *

An hour later as they lay quietly in bed, their breathing slowing down to normal, he covered the back of her hand with his palm. "I hope you're feeling satisfied."

"Actually, I'm not."

He promptly raised his upper body on his elbows, obviously taken aback by her response. "You're not?"

"No. I'm craving a cigarette so bad I can taste it."

He leaned back and enjoyed a big belly laugh, and she joined in.

Chapter 25

What'd I Say?

Sunday morning Monique and Mac made love again, then went to IHOP for breakfast, both of them observing that the pancakes weren't as good as the ones Connie made.

They returned to Mac's, relaxing with the Sunday paper and listening to jazz on the radio in their newly intimate, quiet companionable way, but the serenity was soon interrupted by the arrival of Mac's remaining sibling, Germaine, as well as a return visit from his sister Cora, who came to visit an hour apart, and both of whom brought their families along.

Monique was disappointed by their arrival. She and Mac planned to leave in the early afternoon, just a few hours from now. Now it didn't look like they'd get to spend any time alone together. Hell, the way things were going she should be grateful that no one rang the bell or called while they were making love.

Mac's family members finally left, but half an hour before they were scheduled to hit the road the doorbell rang yet again. Donna, Jerome, and Shaun came by to tell them good-bye, and Jerome asked to speak with Mac privately. Monique was certain it had something to do with Adrian. She cautioned herself against becoming possessive or wanting to be in on everything

Mac did just because she and Mac had slept together. Jerome might have told Mac something in confidence. It not, maybe Mac would choose to share it with her, but if he didn't, she resolved not to ask.

"So this is my home, and my hometown. I hope you've enjoyed yourself here," Mac said as he closed the blinds. Their small overnight bags rested by the front door.

"I love your house, Mac, it's so cozy. I've enjoyed myself tremendously."

"Especially last night."

"Especially last night," she agreed. "But, well . . ."

"What is it?"

She felt buoyed by his concern and felt she could be frank. "I was hoping we'd have some time alone together," she confessed. "It seems like every five minutes somebody's ringing your doorbell, and then they want to hang around all day." The sudden hardening of his features made her realize too late that she sounded selfish and childish. And worst of all, it wasn't just anonymous visitors she was complaining about, but his brothers and sisters. She couldn't possibly have used a poorer choice of words. Diplomacy was desperately needed, and quickly. "I mean—"

"I know what you mean," Mac said coldly. "The people ringing my doorbell happen to be my relatives, Monique, members of my family, people I've known all my life. We're linked by blood. I'm the head of the family since our mother died, and I take a genuine interest in what's happening in everyone's life. I believe in keeping the family unit strong, because when it's all said and done, those are the ones you can depend on.

Friends and lovers may come and go," he said with a withering look directly at her, "but family is forever."

She felt as if she'd just shrunk five inches. "Mac, I'm sorry. It just slipped out. I realize now how terrible I sounded. But I certainly didn't mean to insult your family."

"Forget it. Let's just get ready to head back to Washington."

The return drive was unnaturally quiet. Mac spoke about general topics—different sights they saw, a wreck on the other side of Highway 264, amusing billboards—but nothing personal. Monique felt she might as well have been a casual acquaintance he was giving a ride to, or even a hitchhiker, but certainly not his lover.

She made several attempts to explain she hadn't meant to sound so callous, but each time Mac interrupted and said everything was fine. His hard tone said otherwise. Finally she gave up. Once again she'd alienated the man in her life. It was like her ill-fated romance with Skye Audsley all over again, but much deeper this time because she was truly in love. All those months of cultivating a friendship, having it finally lead to the toe-curling intimacy she'd craved so desperately, and now it was gone because of her carelessness. In her heart she feared it was over. He didn't want to see her again.

How could she have been so stupid?

Mac felt like a fool. His initial opinions about people were rarely wrong, but he'd allowed himself to ignore his gut instinct, the one that told him that Monique was the type of woman who wanted 100 percent of any man who showed interest in her, and that she wanted to be the center of attention. She simply wasn't the type to step into the background; she wanted to be front and center. She'd just proven it to him. She resented the visits of his family members because they took his attention away from her.

The realization hurt deeper than he was willing to admit. He'd enjoyed her company over the past weeks. They'd had a lot of fun together, and in the last week especially, since this crisis with Jerome and Adrian, his feelings for her had grown to match the hunger he'd felt from the very beginning. But all along there'd been hints of trouble ahead, hints he'd chosen to ignore that in hindsight were easy to identify. Like the way her upper lip had curled when he asked her to go on the camping trip with Jerome and Shaun. Her expression reminded him of someone who'd bitten into what looked liked an orange slice, only to taste the bitterness of a lemon. Her obvious distaste for the idea should have told him something, but he'd been so willing to accept her explanation that she'd never gone camping before. She'd probably hated every minute of the four days and three nights they'd spent on Cape Hatteras, only pretending to enjoy it just so she could get one step closer to snaring him.

Then there was the way she'd sweetly maneuvered him into attending the luncheon following her aunt's funeral, when he really needed to get back to work that was already behind schedule. One look at her beautiful, earnest face and he'd gladly allowed himself to be persuaded, but he'd never quite forgotten that triumphant little smile she'd flashed, like she never doubted for a minute that she'd be able to cajole him into doing exactly what she wanted.

How dare she suggest his family was a nuisance? He'd known her exactly four months. *Four months.* She had no right to object to his devotion to the siblings he'd known all his life. He was there when each of his brothers and sisters was brought home from the hospital as infants, and he was also there after they grew up and started having children of their own. He'd been there for Paul and Germaine when their marriages broke up, and for Donna when her husband was killed and when she required assistance during her flares of lupus.

Damn! Just when he thought he and Monique had something special, just when he thought he was falling for her, she showed her true personality, the one he suspected from the start but had convinced himself didn't exist.

His fingers gripped the steering wheel, his mouth set in a hard line. He might feel like a jerk for having fallen for her act, but better to find out about it sooner than later.

Chapter 26

Tomorrow Is Another Day

Monique stifled a yawn. She felt sleepy, in spite of the deafening music that filled the large room. All this noise with that loud, thumping bass wouldn't be enough to keep her awake for another half hour. But when Liz invited her to the dance someone was giving at a country club in Greenville, she hadn't refused. Going out was definitely better than sitting at home moping.

Mac hadn't made his intentions clear to her until they arrived back at the bed-and-breakfast. "Thanks for coming with me, Monique," he said stiffly. "I'm sorry my family made your weekend so unbearable."

She'd merely shaken her head wordlessly, knowing it was hopeless. She'd crossed the line, and he wouldn't forgive her. She could still hear his impersonal parting comment when he dropped her bag inside the front door. "See you around," he'd said. It frequently echoed in her ears, especially at night.

Nearly two weeks had passed since the disastrous trip. Two long weeks without any contact from Mac. She'd written him a brief note of apology, knowing she could do no more. She knew she'd been wrong, but she wasn't about to grovel.

The note had done no good. Mail within the city limits was delivered in one day. He would have called by now if he was going to. She had to accept that she'd failed. The break was complete. Maybe she hadn't been ready to date again after all. If she'd held out getting involved with him a little longer, made sure her tendency to blurt out what she was thinking was truly under control, then maybe . . .

On the other hand, Liz had called a few days after the weekend in Raleigh. "I'm feeling ashamed of myself, Monique," she said. "My own daughter pointed out to me what an absolute jerk I'm being. I'm sorry for the things I said. You were right; I was just looking for someone to blame, and you were available. I hope you can forgive me."

Monique readily accepted her cousin's apology. It was good to have Liz back in her life, but regardless of this she couldn't shake the uncomfortable feeling that Liz was secretly gloating over the breakup with Mac. Still, Liz had been good to her, doing what she could to help keep Monique's mind off of Mac. They met for lunch, they went to the movies. They even joined a bowling league that would be competing every Tuesday starting the week after Labor Day, prompting Monique to wonder if Adrian's comment had gotten Liz to consider other activities other than husband-hunting.

In spite of making up with Liz, when Monique felt she needed someone's ear to confide in about Mac it was Connie she sought out. "I think my mind was running even faster than my mouth, if that's possible," she lamented to her friend one day over breakfast. "Here I was, all ready to ask if you'd be willing to make breakfast for the guests on an occasional weekend in exchange for time off during the week. That way I could go off to

Raleigh with Mac and not feel like I'm saddling Uncle Teddy." Connie's breakfast burritos were a special favorite of hers. With just a sprinkling of chopped cooked ham with a single scrambled egg and sautéed green pepper, the tortillas were particularly diet friendly.

"Frankly, I'm surprised Mac hasn't come around by now," Connie said. "Granted, what you said was thoughtless—"

Monique winced.

"—but you two have built a pretty strong friendship." She shook her head sadly. "I just wish you'd stopped and thought about what you were about to say before you said it. It's a hell of a hard way to find out blood's thicker than water."

"I know."

"But if you ever need to take a weekend off, I'd be happy to fill in for Teddy." Connie reached out to pat her arm. "He's been spending a lot of time at Reggie's lately. I wonder if he's met a new lady friend over there in Charlotte."

"He hasn't mentioned it, and nothing's changed here. He and Mrs. Morgan still get together once or twice a week. Sometimes I eat with them."

"Mrs. Morgan is a friend, period. I'm wondering if he's met someone who's really special to him, someone he might feel attracted to."

"I don't know, but it seems awfully soon for that." Monique sighed. Much as she loved Teddy, she didn't feel like discussing his love life. "Thanks for offering to fill in, Connie. Not that I think I'll be going anywhere with Mac. But a trip to see my parents wouldn't be a bad idea. I haven't seen them since Aunt Peggy died, and I haven't been to New York since last year."

"Monique, has Teddy ever mentioned what his plans

are regarding the B-and-B?" Connie asked. "I mean, it's not like you're going to be here in Washington forever."

Monique appreciated Connie tactfully not pointing out that with Mac out of the picture she now had little reason to stay. "Actually, we did talk about that. He said he'd probably sell. It just about broke my heart when he said it's no fun anymore without Aunt Peggy." She noticed Connie's thoughtful expression. "Why? You interested in buying it?"

"I might just do that."

Monique's eyes widened. She'd only been kidding. "Really, Connie?"

"Sure. It's a nice little business. It gives you plenty of free time, yet you're around people. Best of all, I can do it all myself."

"By yourself?"

"Yes. I can tell that surprises you."

"It does. You seem so family-oriented. I can't picture you wanting to run your own business."

"Being family-oriented was my problem. Don't get me wrong, Monique. I loved Charles, but after he died I suddenly realized I had built my whole life around him and Glenn. I really had no outside interests. I think if I had, it would've made the transition from wife to widow a little easier for me. Charles left me well taken care of financially, but there's more to life than money."

Connie crossed her arms over her chest and rubbed her palms up and down her arms, as if she were cold. "I'll never forget how empty I felt, how depressing it was to wake up to another long, empty day stretching out in front of me." She smiled ruefully. "In hindsight I think I was on the verge of a breakdown. When Glenn was around I'd be all smiles because I didn't want him to worry about me. Then when he'd leave I'd break down and cry and go back to bed. I never want to feel that way again. Owning a bed-and-breakfast would guarantee that. Besides, you can never go wrong with owning real estate." She shrugged. "If I decide I don't want to clean rooms anymore I can always hire someone just like me."

"That's impossible, Connie," Monique said warmly. "You're one in a million."

Now Monique sat in the large banquet room, feeling alone despite the large number of people present, fighting the temptation to cover her ears and the longing for a cigarette. She didn't even carry a pack with her anymore, but she could always bum one from somebody.

She was glad she'd insisted on driving her own car. Liz had spent most of the evening dancing and provided little company. Monique was beginning to feel like the proverbial bump on a log. She'd make an early exit.

"Oo-wee, it's hot in here," Liz said as she dropped her petite frame on a chair. "Haven't you been dancing?"

"Oh, sure. I just decided to sit this one out. You know, give my feet a rest." Monique was too embarrassed to admit the truth. She'd noticed it ever since she'd returned from Raleigh. The near-magical spell she had cast over men since her arrival in Washington had suddenly dissolved, and now no one felt she merited as much as a second glance. At first she attributed it to having left Washington, but when she remembered the camping trip to Hatteras she knew it was all related to the breakup with Mac. Her charmed period had dissolved along with their relationship.

The lone man who asked her to dance tonight was rather sloppy-looking, and she turned him down. She'd rather be a wallflower than dance with a slob. It would be like wearing a sign: *This is the best I could get.*

Soon she and Liz were joined by a man Liz had danced with earlier. While he was on the dance floor Monique thought he was quite handsome. That impression hadn't changed, but close up she could tell he was in his late twenties, maybe thirty at the most. She jabbed Liz's arm after being introduced to him. "Isn't he rather young for you?" she mouthed.

Liz waved her off dismissively, and Monique smiled for the first time that evening.

That simple action made her feel better, more interested in her surroundings. Her eyes scanned the center of the room, where dancing was taking place. It was actually a rather nice party. Her fears about being much older than the rest of the clientele had proved to be unfounded. Many of those present appeared to be at least thirty-five. The discs being spun catered to the more mature crowd. A few recent hits that weren't too unbearable to her ears, both music and lyricwise, were mixed in with classic R&B numbers.

Her breathing suspended temporarily, then came out in short spurts, when she recognized Mac. He wore a gold tweed sports coat and brown slacks and was dancing with a statuesque woman. They were smiling at each other. Looking at them made her feel ill.

She grabbed her purse. "I'm leaving, Liz."

"What?"

"I told you I probably wouldn't stay long."

"Monique, you've been here an hour. I expected you'd leave before I did, but it's not even eleven o'-

clock yet. This wasn't worth the time it took for you to get dressed and drive over here."

She didn't feel like arguing. "Liz, you don't need to worry about how I spend my time. I'm a big girl, and I'm leaving now. Good night."

Simply turning her back on Mac and his dance partner did nothing to relieve the feeling of a dozen daggers plunging into her chest. She could still picture them laughing together. But when she got outside the image suddenly vanished along with the throbbing bass in her head, replaced with only wonder at the beauty of a summer night. She opened her moon roof, put a soothing jazz CD on, and enjoyed the stars in the sky as she drove back to Washington.

Mac was out of her life.

It was time to get over it.

Chapter 27

Daydreaming

"Yes, Mom, I'll be there Saturday," Monique said into the phone. "No, I'd much rather drive . . . Taking the train is too much trouble, and I'd have to drive to Raleigh or Richmond to get a flight to New York. If I can do that I might as well drive all the way up there. This way I'll have my car with me and can drive out to the beach or any other place I want to go without having to borrow your car or Daddy's . . . You know how particular both of you are. God forbid I get any sand on your carpets . . . I know it's a long drive, but I'll be fine . . . All right. See you in a few days." Monique hung up.

She found herself anticipating her trip. She hadn't been home to the Bronx since sometime last year. She usually went for Christmas, but of course they'd all spent that holiday here in Washington with Peggy. The time was right for a trip home. After months of determining which suggestions by her writers' group had merit and rewriting accordingly, she was putting the finishing touches on her manuscript. The data she'd collected on various publishers' submission policies suggested it would be better if she had an agent. One more read-through of the first three chapters and she'd approach five or ten at a time. Surely someone would feel her work had promise. In the meantime, the time had come for her to start thinking of the next phase of her life. Maybe she'd answer a few classified ads for paralegals. If a potential employer requested to meet her personally she could always take the train up for a quick stay.

She might have failed in her goal to triumph over her personality tendencies, but she'd been successful to a point. And while she was seeing Mac she'd been too busy having a good time to wonder where they were headed, or worse, ask him where *he* thought they were headed. She'd blown a few promising relationships that way. She realized now that men didn't like that question, it made them feel boxed in. Just because a woman was over a certain age and feared investing too much time in a man without a resultant marriage didn't give her the right to nag him about his intentions so early on. But she understood it was a question borne out of panic. She had never asked it of any man until after the two years she spent with Austin. She'd been so hurt when he told her he was in love with someone else, and that his feelings for her didn't go any deeper than that of a good friend.

Her impatient nature was largely gone in most aspects. She was more likely to let a driver struggling to change lanes get in front of her, even if it meant having to sit through another red light. She might express mild annoyance but no longer got all worked up when the person in the checkout line in front of her had an item with no price and she had to wait for a runner to find out how much it was. She knew she'd become a better person, but she knew she'd be a lot happier today if only she could have controlled her impatience with regard to Mac's relatives crowding her.

* * *

Mac shook the hands of the couple who had just taken the final walk-through of their new home. They would close this afternoon and move in the following day. Their happiness and excitement were plain to see, and he envied them, young, in love, and starting a new chapter in their lives.

He might no longer be a young man, but he'd known the feeling of being in love. He thought he was safe, thought he hadn't completely fallen for Monique, but now that they were no longer dating he knew better. Her absence from his life created a void he hadn't been able to fill. He spent most of his time trying not to give in to the urge to call her and ask if they could try again, but his common sense convinced him otherwise. He saw nothing but more unhappiness and repeated frustration if he did. In time he'd get over her.

At least that's what he told himself, but thoughts of her filled his mind constantly. He was still daydreaming about their night together while he was helping his crew carry a heavy pipe onto the site of a new home. He was backing up and was so lost in his thoughts he didn't realize he had arrived at the foundation. Someone shouted at him a split second before he went sprawling backward, followed by the most intense pain he had ever had in his life . . . and then nothing.

Monique was in Greenville picking up a few items for her trip when her cell phone rang. She quickly pulled it out of its compartment. "Hello."

"Monique Oliver, please."

"This is she." Her jaw dropped at the caller's next words. "The hospital?" A terrible feeling of foreboding enveloped her entire body. "Did something happen to my uncle?"

"We're actually calling about a Russell McDonald. He gave us your name as a contact. Do you know Mr. McDonald?"

"Mac? Yes, I know him. What happened. Is he all right?"

"He was brought in earlier today after an accident on a construction site. He was struck in the chest by some heavy pipes," the woman continued in a calm manner Monique found infuriating.

"Is he all right?" she repeated.

"He'll be fine, but he's badly bruised, and he has fractures of his sixth and seventh ribs on the right."

"Are you admitting him?"

"Mr. McDonald would prefer to go home, but he informs us he lives alone. Because of the potential for serious problem, even death, if his rib cracks and bone chips get into his bloodstream, it's of utmost importance that he not be left alone. Except for trips to the bathroom he'll require bed rest, and someone will have to bring him meals and perform other activities of daily living for him."

"I'm in Greenville right now, but I'll come right over."

"Fine. I'm in the emergency room, Miss Oliver."

In her eagerness Monique drove as if she were in the Indy 500, leaning forward at her waist and gripping the wheel with both hands. She was at the hospital in eighteen minutes.

At the desk she asked for Mac. She followed the nurse to a curtained area, where Mac lay propped up on a gurney. His rich brown complexion looked a little dull, and he had the exhausted look of someone who'd just had the wind knocked out of him.

The nurse promptly disappeared. Monique whispered a hello. Mac's eyes were closed, and she didn't feel she had to announce her arrival if it meant waking him up.

He opened his eyes and smiled weakly. "Is it really you, or am I still dreaming?"

What did he mean, *still?* "It's me. My goodness, I hope you feel better than you look."

"I don't know. How do I look?"

"Pretty plucking bad," she said with a chuckle. She didn't mean to make fun of him, but she was so glad he was all right.

"I banged up my chest."

"So they told me. How did it happen?"

He sighed deeply, then winced in pain.

"Don't worry about it. You can tell me later."

"I'm so happy you came for me," he said, his eyes still closed and his right hand resting lightly on his chest. His shirt was open, and she saw a tightly fastened elasticized bandage. He opened his eyes and looked directly at her, but he spoke almost shyly. "I didn't know who else to call."

Monique didn't know what to say. Inside she had a half dozen questions she wished she could demand that he answer. *Why didn't you call me before this? Do you have any idea what I've gone through? Would you have called me at all if you hadn't been injured? Now that you* have *contacted me, what does it all mean?* But of course this wasn't the time or the place.

She reached for his hand. She held it in both of hers and squeezed it. "I hope you'll always consider me a friend, Mac," she said honestly.

The nurse returned before Mac could answer. "The doctor will be in to give you discharge instructions shortly," she said. "In the meantime just get some rest."

"Are you sure he's really well enough to go home, nurse?" Monique asked. "He looks like he just went ten rounds with Roy Jones."

"His ribs are going to be sore for a few days. He just needs some bed rest and someone to look after him to keep his movement at a minimum. That doesn't really require hospitalization unless there's no one to help him."

"No hospital," Mac mumbled. "I want to go home. My sister Cora will come to Washington and help if I ask her."

"That won't be necessary, Mac," Monique said. "You'll come home with me."

"To the B-and-B?"

"Yes, of course." But even as she spoke she tried to figure how she'd work it all out. Her four guest rooms were either booked or about to be booked in the busy late summer season, and of course Connie needed time in between reservations to get previously occupied rooms ready for new guests.

Then she hit on a solution. Mac would sleep in her room. She could make a pallet on the floor with quilts and blankets, or even borrow one of his sleeping bags, like she had when they went camping.

"I don't want to be in the way."

"Mac, stop being stubborn. You won't be in the way. Now go ahead and rest, like the nurse said."

He closed his eyes, and when she heard the deep, even breaths of sleep she slipped out to the hall and called her mother to tell her she wouldn't be coming up after all.

Chapter 28

Loose Lips

Monique wasn't surprised when her mother expressed disappointment at the news that she wouldn't be up this weekend, but she calmed at Monique's assurance that she'd get there within the next few weeks.

Getting her mother off the phone was more challenging, for Julia wanted to know all about Mac. "It sounds like things are getting serious between you two," she hinted.

"No, Mom. We're friends. We haven't even seen much of each other the last few weeks. We . . . we had a disagreement, and we kind of broke up."

"You didn't tell me!" It sounded like an accusation.

"Mom, you know I never tell you much about my love life. You take everything to heart too much. When Skye and I got engaged you started knitting baby booties in anticipation."

"There's nothing wrong with a woman my age wanting grandchildren, Monique. I'm the only one in my social circle who doesn't have any. Wait until you're sixty-seven with a forty-year-old daughter, and then you'll know how I feel."

"Okay, Mom." She knew pointing out that she probably wouldn't have children at all would only start her mother on another tangent.

"And this raises another question," Julia continued. "If you two have broken up, what are you doing staying down there to take care of him?"

Her answer came without hesitation. "Because he needed me."

"He's got a lot of nerve, knowing you had plans this weekend and asking you to take care of him anyway. What if you had bought an airline ticket?"

"I didn't buy an airline ticket, Mom, as you know. Besides, he had no idea I had plans. We hadn't been talking, remember?"

"And you just jumped when he called. That's not like you, Monique. Did you do this because you felt sorry for him?"

"No, Mom. There were other people he could have called. His sister from Raleigh would have come to help him, or even the guy who does maintenance at the inn. They're friends."

Julia was silent, a rare moment of speechlessness. "You may *think* you have no definable reason for acting the way you did, Monique, but I know better," she said confidently when she finally spoke. "I know exactly why you're behaving so against character. You think about it for a while. It'll come to you."

"Okay, Mom. Listen, I've got another call to make. Can I call you later? Maybe Daddy'll be home then and I can say hi to him, too."

"Yes, that's fine. Go tend to your duties, Florence Nightingale." Julia laughed.

Monique said good-bye, hung up, and dialed Connie, who was finishing up for the day but agreed to put fresh linens on Monique's bed. As Monique rushed back to Mac's bedside she admired Connie's ability to straddle the very different dual roles of employee and friend. Never before had she asked Connie to change her bed or do anything in her bedroom, but Connie had simply said she would take care of it without asking any questions. Maybe she thought they were about to host a handicapped guest.

Monique returned to Mac's partition just minutes before the doctor came in. He orally went over the instructions for Mac's care at home and gave her a sheet with everything in writing. The doctor informed her that the earliest Mac should go back to work would be Wednesday of next week, and then only with a release from a physician and with strict adherence to light duty for another two weeks.

"All right, we're here," Monique said, using the cheery tone usually directed toward terrified children when arriving at the dentist's office. She shifted the gear to park and turned off the ignition. It only took a minute for her to grab her purse and hop out of the driver's side. By the time she walked around to the passenger side Mac had swung the door open and shifted his body sideways, his feet touching the ground.

"Can you make it?" she asked.

"Yeah, just give me a minute." Holding on to the top of the door frame, he slowly got to his feet, wincing from the pressure of the tight bandage around his chest. "I still think it would be better if you came to my place with me," he said. "All my stuff is there."

"You might be right about that, but since we're here, why don't you relax? I've got to be here to check in an arriving guest. We can always go to your place later." She opened the front door and held it for him, but he gestured for her to go in first.

"Hey!" Connie greeted.

Monique managed a wan smile. She figured Connie would be gone by now. She didn't want Mac to know she had canceled her vacation plans to care for him. If he found out he'd feel terribly guilty and probably insist he could manage on his own, or ask Cora to come down from Raleigh. From what Monique had learned at the hospital, his being alone could be fatal. She couldn't risk his leaving. She *had* to keep Connie from spilling her plans. Like they used to say in the movies, it was a matter of life or death.

"I was just about to leave," Connie was saying. "I wanted to see you before you—"

Monique made a choking sound, but then Connie broke off when she saw Mac. "Hey there," she said, obviously surprised and happy to see him. "Long time, no see."

"Hi, Connie."

Connie's gaze lingered on Mac, undoubtedly sensing something was amiss, but then turned her attention back to Monique. "Don't worry about anything. I've got it all covered."

Monique shook her head frantically, silently mouthing the word "No." Fortunately, Mac had gone ahead and sat in one of the parlor's wing chairs. He still looked a little whipped, but with his shirt buttoned no one could see the bandage beneath.

"That won't be necessary after all, Connie, but I appreciate your wanting to help," Monique said.

Connie immediately looked puzzled. She mouthed, "What happened?"

Monique cleared her throat and gave Connie what she hoped was a threatening stare. "Thanks a lot, Connie. I know you have to go," she said pleasantly, adding in a whisper, "I'll call you later."

After Connie left, Monique decided to make seeing Teddy a priority. After sheer luck had prevented Connie from revealing her plans, how ironic it would be if Teddy stopped by to wish her a safe trip in front of Mac.

She glanced at Mac. "Are you all right?" she said. He looked reasonably comfortable, and the doctor wanted him to sit up as much as possible rather than recline all day.

"Yeah, I'm fine. You go do what you need to do. All I ask is that you bring me back something to eat. A burger will do fine, preferably a double stack. All the stuff they put on it is okay, but instead of mayo I want mustard. No fries."

"Okay, I'll be back shortly. You just sit tight."

"What about your new guest?"

"They aren't due to arrive for over an hour, so I've got a little time."

"You don't think I'll scare the people already staying here, sitting here like this?"

"Of course not. As far as they know you're just another guest. You certainly won't frighten anyone." She chuckled. "If you want to know the truth, you don't look like much of a threat."

Satisfied, he promptly leaned his head back and closed his eyes. She stood for a few moments observing him. Mac was here, sitting in her parlor. She never thought she'd enjoy this sight again, but the future was by no means certain. She just wanted to savor the moment. Besides, it wasn't like he knew she was standing there. He'd dozed off already.

As she watched him so fondly she remembered what her mother had said. She'd been right, it certainly wasn't like her to forget all about what she had planned for the sake of a man. If anything, she'd expected them to cancel *their* plans for *her*. But with Mac she hadn't hesitated. Sure, she'd felt hurt that he'd stayed away from her these past weeks—she still did—but that wasn't the important thing. He needed her, and she acted instinctively. It wouldn't have been right to ignore him just because he'd ignored her. What was that proverb? Two wrongs don't make a right. Well, they didn't.

Monique blinked. Suddenly she understood. She *loved* Mac. That was why she'd only thought about what he needed and not about the plans she had for the weekend. But this wasn't the type of love she'd felt—or *thought* she'd felt—for Ozzie. Even with him, she had always put herself first.

Tears came to her eyes at the realization of what she had . . . and knowing she might have lost it already. But what mattered most was Mac's well-being, that his ribs heal properly and completely.

She stood and gazed at him for several more minutes, then wiped her eyes with her wrist and went toward the kitchen, intending to slip out the back door so Mac wouldn't be jolted by the sound of the heavy front door closing.

As soon as she left Mac opened his eyes and looked thoughtfully in the direction she had gone.

Chapter 29

True Confession

Monique spoke with Teddy for a few minutes, then went and picked up two hamburgers. She was back at the B&B in thirty-five minutes.

Mac was still sitting where she left him. The sound of soft breathing paired with the even rise and fall of his chest told her he was more than dozing off, he was fast asleep.

She moved closer. Was that a smile she saw? His lips were turned up ever so slightly at the ends. She wondered if he was dreaming. He hadn't been sleeping long, but she supposed exhaustion could do that to a person.

Monique decided not to wake him. She was hungry herself, and unlike Mac she hadn't skipped the fries. It had been about two weeks since she'd last enjoyed such a calorie-laden meal, and she intended to enjoy it.

She poured herself a glass of grapefruit juice and had just sat at the round drop-leaf butcher block table in a corner of the kitchen when Mac came in. "What's this? Lunch without me?"

"Hey, you were just sleeping a minute ago."

"I must have smelled the food. Nothing like grilled onions to wake up your nose." He opened the refrigerator. "What've you got in here to drink?"

"Grapefruit juice, some orange juice, and some punch."

"No Sprite or Seven-Up?"

"I don't drink soda. Too much sugar."

He took a glass from the cabinet and poured fruit punch into it, then joined her at the table, where he devoured his hamburger in five or six bites. "Wow, that was good. I could eat another one."

"I'll get you another as soon as I'm done. I don't eat as fast as you do."

"No, that's all right. If I eat any more it'll probably make me sick."

"Are you feeling better?"

"My stomach feels great. My chest still hurts like hell." He paused. "Monique . . . I'm sure you had things you wanted to do today. I really feel just awful about keeping you from doing what you wanted, especially since . . . Anyway, it was really good of you to come right to the hospital for me. It's more than I have any right to expect, and I know it." He held up a hand palm out when she opened her mouth to say something. "No, let me finish. I know I should have called you after we got back from Raleigh. I'll tell you the truth. I've never stopped thinking of you. Lord knows I tried to. I've hung out more in the last few weeks than I have in the last two years, hoping I could keep you out of my mind."

She remembered him dancing with that woman at the country club in Greenville. He'd certainly looked like he was having fun then, she thought. But she couldn't hold that against him, not when he said he had kept busy simply to try and stop thinking about her.

"What kept me from calling you was that I believed you'd never accept the responsibility I feel for my family," he continued. "I've had that problem before. When my mother was ill I experienced the real meaning of the 'sandwich generation.' We were all having a hard time with it, but Jerome and Shaun were really miserable. They've seen more loss in their young lives than many people twice their age. First their father when they were almost too young to understand what death really means. Then their grandfather, who had been somewhat of a surrogate. That's when I stepped in. Things got so hectic that my girlfriend quit me. I didn't want history to repeat itself, but when you said what you said, I figured it was about to, despite my best efforts to get you to understand. I felt we'd both save ourselves a lot of grief if we stopped seeing each other right then. When I got your letter I thought it would be the least painful if I took the out you offered me."

She had ended her letter to him by saying she would take his silence to mean it was over between them.

"I don't know. Maybe I should have given you an explanation, told you how I felt," Mac mused.

"No," Monique said firmly. "If you'd called after getting my letter I would have thought . . . I would have thought you were calling to make up, not to break it off. You did the right thing. But since we're being truthful with each other, I want you to know something, Mac." She took a deep breath and let the words spill out. "There was a time when I truly wouldn't have felt I'd said anything for you to take offense at. And my reaction to your telling me you'd see me around"—she noticed him wince—"would have been merely that you were too temperamental. Then I would've moved on to my next victim."

"Victim?"

"Yes. What you saw that night in Raleigh was a glimpse of the old me, the one who felt threatened by anyone who took my boyfriend's attention away from me. You see, I was once engaged to a wonderful, successful man, and then I suggested to my fiancé that he consider putting his grandmother—who was his only living relative and who'd raised him after his parents died—in a nursing home."

He looked stunned. "You suggested that under those circumstances? What happened?"

"He was my fiancé, and as you know I've never been married, so there you have it." She shrugged, then decided to go ahead and state the ugly truth aloud. "He broke our engagement right then and there."

"How do you feel about that now?"

"At the time I was more embarrassed than hurt." She suddenly felt a lot better. If she could actually confess the Skye fiasco aloud she knew she'd be all right. Darlene had been right about her; she disliked divulging anything that showed her in an unfavorable light. That was why she'd been so reluctant to admit that Gregory's timing and not losing Gregory himself had upset her the most when he broke up with her just before her birthday and the holidays. She'd viewed Gregory as a mere convenience. If she knew it, Gregory had probably felt it, too. No wonder he jumped at the chance to reconcile with his old girlfriend when he felt the love she still had for him.

Monique turned her thoughts back to Skye. "In hindsight, I realize I never really loved him, I just told myself I did," she said to Mac. "He was good-looking, he was successful, and he adored me. I went after him on the rebound, after I'd been cut loose by the man I really loved in favor of someone else. It seemed like a good way to show him up." She met his eyes with a frank, unashamed stare. "I really wasn't a very nice person then, Mac. But something happened last year that forced me to admit something was wrong. I'd never learned to look outside the box of my own convenience. I've always been catered to. I'm an only child, and I've pretty much always gotten whatever I wanted. Somewhere along the way I lost consideration for other people. My wishes were the only thing that counted, and everything else had become secondary." She saw a flicker of some unidentifiable emotion in his eyes. Could it be admiration for recognizing her faults and doing something about it, or did he think she was a miserable excuse for a human being?

She felt an urge to keep talking; it felt therapeutic. "But once I identified what was wrong I've tried very hard not to be so self-centered. I've been analyzing every action I take. I thought I had my old ways beat, but it's difficult, trying to conquer the bad habits of a lifetime. I'm not sure why I said what I did that day, why I felt so threatened by your family. We'd had such a wonderful weekend, and then I ruined it with my big mouth."

"Maybe I was too hard on you, Monique."

"You're just being nice, but I think that's sweet of you."

At Monique's suggestion he went into her room to relax after they ate. The Vicodin he'd been given at the hospital was wearing off, but Monique insisted it wasn't yet time to take two more, that he had to wait a full six hours. He lay with his upper body propped up and tried not to think about how much it hurt.

His thoughts turned to that weekend in Raleigh, where his relationship with Monique had gone from good to better to bust. He couldn't help thinking that maybe she hadn't been all that unreasonable to expect more of his attention. He'd told her she'd meet some of his large family while they were in town, but in fact she'd met all of them, plus much of the next generation, his nieces and nephews. Even he hadn't expected to see all his siblings and most of their children. He asked himself honestly if he would have felt just a little incensed if the tables had been turned and a stream of Monique's family members dropped by all day long and into the evening the very first time she'd invited him home with her. Wouldn't he have felt miffed if this pattern continued the morning after they made love for the first time? He'd been hoping himself that they could spend some time alone together to adjust to the intimate turn their friendship had taken, but they'd hardly had time to pick up the newspaper before Germaine and Cora showed up with their kids and Cora's husband.

Mac loved his family. He was glad he'd had the opportunity to catch up with all of them. This was, after all, the first time he'd seen many of them since Easter. But on the same token, he couldn't really blame Monique for expecting the weekend to take a different course. All right, so she could have used better phrasing. The way she put it sounded like someone only concerned with what she wanted, just like she'd said. But now he understood it. Under the circumstances it wasn't the unpardonable sin he originally felt it was.

He gingerly touched his bandaged chest. Sometimes things had a funny way of working out. His coworkers told him he'd been unresponsive for about fifteen seconds after the pipe knocked him down. After he had convinced himself of all the reasons why he shouldn't call her, it had taken an injury that literally knocked him unconscious to get him to act. He'd be forever grateful to her for being there for him.

And now that she was back in his life, he wasn't about to let her get away from him again.

Chapter 30
Priorities

She heard him call out to her uncertainly in the darkness. "Monique?"

"I'm here." She hastily got to her feet to stand at his bedside.

"We're still at the B-and-B?"

"Yes. You fell asleep. I didn't want to wake you to bring you back to your place. You can shower and brush your teeth in the morning."

"Where are you sleeping?"

"I took some old quilts and made a pallet on the floor."

The way his features wrinkled told her how little he thought of that idea. "I don't want you sleeping on the floor because I'm taking up your bed. You come to bed. I'll sleep on the damn floor."

"There's no reason to swear, Mac."

"Never mind my language," he said stubbornly. "I won't have you sleeping on the floor, Monique."

"It's very comfortable. It's just like sleeping on a really firm mattress. Besides, there's nowhere else to sleep. All four rooms upstairs are booked. I can't run the risk of letting one of the guests see me sleeping on the parlor sofa. This is a respectable bed-and-breakfast, not a flophouse."

"Come get in bed with me."

"Mac!"

"Relax. I'm not asking you for sex. Not that I wouldn't like it," he added after a brief pause, "but I hurt too much. After all you've done for me it's just not right for you to be sleeping on the floor. Come on, I'll help you." He used his elbows to awkwardly move into a sitting position. The cover fell away, exposing that he wore nothing but his elasticized chest bandage and boxer shorts.

Monique almost gasped aloud. Only now did she notice his shirt and jeans neatly folded on the chair. Having a view of so much of his muscular, toned body reminded her of the night in Raleigh when they had made love, and how much she missed his embrace, his touch, his weight atop her. She knew it would be futile to object. She needed to get him to cover up so she could forget about his physique and squelch the memories of that one heavenly night they spent together. "You lie down. I'll get these things out of the way."

After moving the linens to a corner, she placed her pillow on the bed and then gingerly lowered her weight onto the mattress, not wanting his chest to be jostled. She wore a bright pink sleep shirt imprinted with an image of Betty Boop, chosen because the crew neckline and just-above-the-knee length was the most unsexy sleepwear she owned. But suddenly it didn't matter that she was wearing something more appropriate for a girl Adrian's age. She was in bed with the man she loved, and her emotions were unclothed even if her body wasn't. Her heart ached to reach out and touch him, but she couldn't. He'd been the one to reject her, and now he had to make the first move, if there would be one.

But whatever happened, she would never regret postponing her trip to New York.

Mac lay on his back, his upper body propped up with pillows. He could feel Monique climb into bed beside him. He knew she was trying to be careful, but nevertheless the slight movement of the mattress made him grimace in pain. He stifled a groan. He wanted her to sleep peacefully, not worry about him.

Her leg brushed against his in the small double bed. In an instant she pulled it back, as if he had burned her or something. "I'm sorry," she whispered.

He could stand it no longer. "Monique, honey, I'm not made of glass."

"I just want it to be like . . . like I'm not even here."

"But you *are* here." Every muscle in his body was acutely aware of that, one muscle in particular. What he wouldn't give to be able to reach out and stroke her thigh, her firm belly, and the heavenly area between. Trying not to think about her lying so close to him would probably keep him up all night. "I'm just glad I woke up when I did so I could keep you from spending all night on the floor." That was it. He had to be noble.

"Mac, I told you it was all right."

He was too busy thinking about something that had been bothering him to reply right away. Now was the time to ask her. If her reply made him feel even more worthless, he supposed he had it coming. "Monique . . . I'm going to ask you something, and I want you to tell me the truth. Did you have plans to take a trip this weekend?"

When he heard her gasp he had his answer.

"My goodness, how did you know?"

"There was a suitcase in front of your closet the first time I came into this room earlier today. When I woke up it was gone. You canceled your plans for me?"

She'd realized too late that she hadn't asked Connie to put her partially packed suitcase back in her closet. She had slipped in while he was asleep and quietly put it away, hoping he'd think nothing of it or maybe not even remember having seen it. She could tell him she'd merely been rearranging her closet, but he'd asked for honesty. "I felt it was the right thing to do, Mac. I have no regrets."

He felt a dull ache in his stomach, that sickening feeling people get when they realize they've been terribly wrong. "Now I really feel like a first-class heel. I've treated you badly, Monique. I had no right to tell the hospital to call you. I couldn't have blamed you if you'd told me tough luck and gone about your business. I should have just called Cora. Her family could've gotten along without her for a few days. Hell, I could even have called Lyman and asked to bunk on his sofa. Connie would've probably been around enough to make sure I didn't keel over." He'd actually given the latter serious thought. Even though both Connie and Lyman had been good friends to him and most likely would have rushed to his aid, in the end he decided he didn't want to be a third wheel. Lyman spoke of Connie with such tenderness, anyone could see he was in love with her. He often said how fortunate he considered himself to have gotten her to go out with him first after a decent interval had passed since her husband's death. Mac didn't have the heart to point out that Connie probably didn't have men beating a path to her front door, the way Monique did.

"Where were you going, if you don't mind my asking?" he asked Monique.

"I was just taking a drive up to New York for a few days to visit with my parents and maybe catch up with some friends, do some job hunting. It's nothing I can't do at a later time. There's no canceled reservations or fees or anything like that involved. It's done. You should just forget it."

"I can't tell you how grateful I am to you for staying here with me. Tell you what," he said. "When I'm all healed up, say the weekend after next, I'll drive up with you. We'll have dinner, see a show, visit people, and we can even stay in the city rather than with your parents if you think that's best. Would you like that?"

"I'd love it, but you don't have to feel obligated."

"It's not that, Monique. I'd be lying if I said I didn't feel a huge load of guilt about your sacrifice, but I also realize how foolish I've been. You did something today that was both extremely kind and completely unselfish." Mac reached for her hand under the covers and covered it with his. "I already know how much I've missed being with you. What we had in Raleigh was special. I've been thinking about it ever since, even more than I've thought about what transpired the next day."

Again Monique felt a need to address that terrible day. But now she felt a lot better about it because he'd just said he wanted them to get past it, that he didn't want to end their relationship over it. "I know family is important to you, Mac. It's just that I've never really had any responsibilities for anyone other than myself. My parents are healthy, thank God. And while my aunt was ill, she had Teddy and Reggie—that's my cousin—to take care of her. I can't imagine offering emotional support to so many people the way you do. I admire you for it."

He rolled onto his side and reached out for her. "C'mere, baby."

She carefully shifted from her stomach to her side, facing him. "Mac—"

"It's all right. As much as I'd love to make love to you right now, I'm just hurting too badly. But I can't stand having you this close and not touching you."

"You're sure I'm not in your way?"

"Never." He settled in comfortably, his arm around her waist, his face close to hers, and closed his eyes. A moment later he felt her palm lightly grip his biceps muscle. Perfect. Not only did he have a pressing need to feel her flesh beneath his hand, his need to feel her touch was just as strong.

He lay awake, savoring Monique's closeness, long after she fell asleep. He had slept most of the day just to escape from the pain of his bruised ribs, and even after taking another Motrin he wasn't sleepy. After what seemed like hours, he finally felt himself drifting off.

His last conscious thought was how good it felt to have a woman in his life who would drop everything to run to him simply because he needed her.

Chapter 31

Wonderful Town

Monique beamed as Mac answered her mother's questions, which she knew had been carefully phrased to extract as much information from him as possible. From what she could tell, both her parents were pleased with the man she'd brought home to meet them. She'd cautioned her mother that she and Mac were just good friends, but her mother had a way of forgetting anything inconvenient or unpleasant. And Monique couldn't deny that it felt good to have them approve of Mac, even if the future of their relationship was still uncertain.

"Seven children!" Julia exclaimed. "What a crowded house you must have had."

"It could be inconvenient when someone was in the bathroom," Mac replied, "but overall it was kinda nice, always having somebody to play with or go someplace with. We didn't have a whole lot of material things, but we were well fed, got good medical and dental care, and we had lots of love."

"That's all children need," Frank Oliver said, nodding approval. "If you ask me, kids today have too much. When I was coming up a piece of chalk and a sidewalk could keep us entertained all afternoon."

"I know what you mean, Mr. Oliver. We had two televisions, one in my parents' bedroom and the other in living room, that all of us had to share. Now kids feel their lives aren't complete unless they have their own telephone, television, computer, stereo, and Gameboy. They don't know anything about sharing."

"I never had to share," Monique said with a smile.

"An only child never does," Mac answered.

"We never meant for our Monique to be an only child," Julia said, a little sadness in her voice. "It just worked out that way."

"She was the light of our lives," Frank added. He looked at Monique lovingly. "Still is."

After dinner Monique helped her mother clear the table. Munching on the last biscuit, she loaded the dishwasher while her mother wrapped and put away the pork roast, green beans, and macaroni and cheese. Mac and her father adjourned to the living room to watch the remainder of the local news.

"I like him, Monique," Julia said enthusiastically. "Daddy does, too. I can tell. There's nothing like a good southern boy with a good old-fashioned upbringing. I always hoped you'd find someone in North Carolina. Atlanta might be in the South, but it's strictly geographic. From what I understand everybody down there is from up here."

"Mom, you're forgetting what I told you. Mac and I are friends. Good friends, but friends."

"You're sleeping together, aren't you?"

"Mom!"

"All right, I'll rephrase. Do you have one hotel room or two?"

She sighed. "One, Mom, if you must know." She didn't know why she felt so shy all of a sudden. After all, she was forty years old. "It's a long story. We broke up for a few weeks"—that was all it had been, though it seemed like so much longer—"and we're just getting back together. This trip has the potential to be a significant turning point for us, but it's too early to know." Mac had seen the doctor yesterday and been completely cleared for a return to normal activity, including, she presumed, sex. "We just got into town a few hours ago, and this was our first stop. It was sweet of you to have dinner for us."

"We wouldn't have missed the chance to meet Mac, dear."

Monique and Mac waved to the Olivers as they drove off, headed for their accommodations in midtown Manhattan. "Nice people," Mac commented.

"They're the best."

"I feel the same about my parents."

She looked at him, not sure of what to say. "You miss them, don't you?"

"Yes, but I know I'm doing as they would have wanted. Looking out for my brothers and sisters, and helping out however I can. If someone's gone that's about the only comfort you can get, besides your memories."

Monique's thoughts automatically went to Peggy, and she understood precisely what Mac meant. Somehow she knew Peggy would approve of what she'd struggled so hard to accomplish.

Mac surprised Monique by booking them not into a hotel, but a bed-and-breakfast on a quiet Upper East Side Street, just steps from Central Park. "After staying at Dodson's Bed-and-Breakfast in Washington, I don't think I'll ever stay at another hotel again," he said as he pulled over in front of a handsome redbrick town house.

"Are you sure this is it? There's no sign out front."

"They're very low-key in this neighborhood. They wouldn't even give me their address until I gave them a deposit with my credit card."

"There's nowhere to park," she observed.

"They told me there's a garage on the next street. Why don't I let you out with the bags and get you inside, and then I'll be right over? We won't need the car until we're ready to leave."

The innkeepers were waiting for them to check in. As they sat in the sunny antique-furnished parlor, Monique told the married couple that she also ran a bed-and-breakfast, and they exchanged tips. Mac looked over the credit card charges, signed the bill, and was given a set of keys.

Monique paused in front of the stairs, garment bag slung over her shoulder, eager to see their room and how it compared to the rooms at Dodson's. "Where are you going?" she asked when Mac, holding their small weekend bags in each hand, went to the front door.

"Downstairs to our apartment."

"Apartment?"

"Don't ask," he said good-naturedly. "Just follow me."

The ground-floor apartment—a half flight down from street level by outside stairs—was charming, with walls painted a dusky rose and stuffed floral furniture and heavy oak accent tables. "Mac, this is lovely!" Monique exclaimed, running a hand over the round oak dining room table, which had already been set with place mats, stoneware, stainless steel, glassware, and napkins in service for four. "The table is set for four. Are there two bedrooms?"

"Only one. The other apartment is a studio. But the sofa bed opens into a bed and can sleep two more."

"It's nice for families visiting New York," she remarked. "But we really didn't need all this, our own private kitchen and all. A bed and bath would have been fine."

"Rest assured, I didn't get this because I expect you to cook, Monique. It's just that I didn't want to run into other guests the minute we opened the door and stepped into the hall or onto the stairs," he said, moving closer. He took her hand and brought it to his face, rubbing the back of it against his cheek. "I wanted complete privacy for us. Do you want to know why?"

She smiled at him with all the love in her heart. "I think I already know. Let's take advantage of it."

Hours later, after Mac proved to Monique that he was completely healed and they lay together in the dark, he put an arm around her and said, "I want you to know I really didn't plan for this to happen so quickly, literally as soon as we walked in. I thought we would inspect the room and then go for a walk."

"A walk? In the *park*?"

"No, of course not. I thought we'd walk around the neighborhood, maybe stop somewhere for a drink. I guess now it's too late. I hope you don't mind."

"No, Mac. I'm just where I want to be." With a wicked smile she added, "I'd rather hoped we'd be able to get to bed early."

"Mac, this is so great," Monique said amid the buzz of voices during the theater intermission. "I just love Brian

Stokes Mitchell's voice. I caught him in *Man of La Mancha* last year, and he was wonderful. Good-looking, too."

"Watch that."

"Oh, c'mon, you know I wouldn't trade you in for him. If anything, I'd want someone younger, like that fine Morris Chestnut," she joked.

"I enjoy the theater. I don't get to New York as often as I'd like to. We got pretty good seats, too, considering I just ordered the tickets on Tuesday."

"That's because it's low season," she said. "Everybody's trying to get out of New York during the dog days of August, not come here."

"But you don't mind being here now, do you?"

"Of course not. I'd planned to come up two weeks ago, remember? I was just talking about how theater attendance tends to drop this time of year. It'll pick up again in the fall." She looked around eagerly. She loved being part of a well-dressed crowd. This was her New York, the New York of glittering, stylish, elegant nightlife, leisurely al fresco meals after dark, and accommodations in a chic town house on the Upper East Side, just steps away from Fifth Avenue and Central Park. Even in the stifling summer heat of August, it felt good to be home again.

"Excuse me. Monique?"

Her eyes widened in astonishment. She recognized the voice, but part of her couldn't believe it was him. She turned her head, and her surprise was genuine. "Ozzie! I don't believe it! Imagine bumping into you, of all people!"

He bent and kissed her cheek. "You're looking wonderful, Monique."

"Thank you. So are you." She spoke the truth. Ozzie had the look of a happy, contented man.

"Thanks." He took the hand of the regal woman standing next to him, her natural hair brushed into a French roll. "Monique, you remember my wife, Desirée."

"Of course. Hello, Desirée. How nice to see you again." Desirée smiled and returned the greeting.

Mac had been hanging back a little, but Monique linked her right arm through his left and pulled him forward. "Mac, I want you to meet an old friend of mine, Austin Hughes, and his wife, Desirée. Ozzie, Desirée, Mac McDonald."

Mac said hello and shook their hands.

"I'm so surprised to see them because they live out in Colorado now," Monique explained to Mac. She looked at Ozzie curiously. "You two haven't returned to New York to live, have you?"

"No. We were surveying a few hotels in the New York/New Jersey area this month, and we're taking some time out for a minivacation," Ozzie explained.

"The kids are with Ozzie's parents in Westchester," Desirée added.

Ozzie pulled out his wallet and proudly showed Monique and Mac photos of their preschool-age son and toddler daughter. "What a lovely family," Monique said sincerely.

"What about you, Monique?" Ozzie asked. "Are you back in New York?"

"No. I was in Atlanta until last year, when I moved to North Carolina. Do you remember Washington, my mother's hometown?" She glanced at Mac, thinking she'd felt him go rigid beside her, but he quickly waved her off.

"Oh, yes!" Ozzie nodded. "Picturesque little place. I didn't think it was your type of setting, though. Too quiet."

"I'm enjoying my time there. I don't expect to be there the rest of my life, but right now it's just what I need. Mac and I are just up for the weekend. We saw my parents—"

"Please give them my best."

"I will. Have you seen Zack?"

"Yes. He still lives in his brownstone up in Harlem. We spent our first night in town with him and his wife. You don't know Vivian, do you?"

"No, we never met."

"She's a sweetheart," Desirée said. "Our kids are all great friends."

The theater lights dimmed momentarily, indicating that intermission was nearly over.

"Please give my regards to everyone, your parents and Zack," Monique said to Ozzie.

"Will do."

They all said good-bye, with Mac shaking Ozzie's hand once more and exchanging a polite nod with Desirée. "Imagine that," Monique mused. "Coming to New York and seeing some people I know from two-thirds of the way across the country."

"They looked like a nice couple," Mac said. "I, uh, couldn't help noticing you seemed to know him better than you do her. He's been to Washington with you?"

She smiled. So that was why he'd suddenly gotten stiff. He was actually jealous! How cute. "He was an old boyfriend. It was over a long time ago." Funny. While she'd mentioned their relationship in her confession to Mac the other week, she hadn't really given Ozzie any deep thought in months. Was it really as recently as last Christmas that she was lamenting the end of their love affair? Now that she'd seen him, she only felt happiness for him. He and Desirée were obviously very much in love.

"I guess so," Mac said, "since their son looked like he's four or five years old. Was he the one you didn't love, the one you got involved with after someone else dumped you?"

"No," she answered with a matter-of-factness that surprised her. "He was the one I loved, the one who dumped *me*." She met his gaze head-on, and just before the curtain rose she added in a whisper, "But that was then. *You're* the one I love now."

Chapter 32
I Do! I Do!

Fourteen months later

Monique beamed as she and Mac faced their family members and friends. She and Mac had just taken their vows and shared their first kiss as husband and wife. They stood for a few moments, reveling in the applause of their loved ones who shared their bliss. Liz adjusted Monique's headpiece, and she and Mac led the rest of the bridal party out of the church and into the autumn afternoon.

The bridal party, including maid of honor Liz, Connie, Adrian, Gina, the wife of her cousin Reggie, Mac's niece Shaun, Mac's sister Germaine, best man Jerome, groomsmen Reggie, Lyman, and Mac's brothers Michael and Paul, went for a photo session while the guests headed directly for the reception in the banquet room of a seafood restaurant on the banks of the Pamlico River. By the time they arrived the cocktail hour was in full swing.

"Monique, you're absolutely radiant," Diane Winston said when she reached the front of the receiving line. "Your dress is lovely."

"Thanks, Diane." Monique looked down at the white satin gown with its tight bodice and simple A-line skirt.

"I had to do a lot of searching to find something suitable for a first-time bride of forty-one." Monique chuckled, then shook the hand of Diane's husband. "Hello, Arthur."

"I wish you and Mac all the happiness in the world, Monique."

"Thank you so much."

"I don't think you've met our daughter, Sabrina. She missed the big dance, both this year and last."

"Hello, Sabrina. So nice to meet you."

"Nice to meet you, Mrs. McDonald."

"Ooh, you lovely girl, I'll never forget you," Monique said with an excited squeal. "You're the very first person to call me 'Mrs. McDonald'!" She hugged the young woman. In spite of her happiness she found herself wondering why Sabrina, who had not been included on her parents' invitation, was here in the first place, but when she recognized the young man standing beside Sabrina, who had been invited to bring a date, it all fell into place.

"Glenn! Is that you?"

"It's me, Miss Monique."

As Monique embraced him she remembered Connie speculating last year that Glenn had special feelings for Sabrina. How wonderful to see the two of them together. On this, her wedding day, she wanted the whole world to be in love, and there was something especially heart-rendering about young love.

Like that of Jerome and Adrian, whom she could see standing together a little further down the line. Jerome had begun his second year at Shaw, and Adrian was now a freshman at Elizabeth City State. The former underage lovers were now eighteen and nineteen, still young, but adults in the eyes of the law, free to express their love for each other, a love that to everyone's surprise had not diminished over the last fifteen months, most of which time they'd been forcibly separated. They might not have been partnered for the walk down the aisle—as best man, Jerome had escorted Liz—but Monique wondered if they would eventually walk down the aisle as bride and groom themselves.

Liz had felt uncomfortable with the idea of being escorted by "a fellow young enough to be my son . . . and who one day might well *become* my son!" Her trepidation was soon forgotten when she met Mac's brother Paul, who at thirty-eight was a divorcé. From what Monique observed, the attraction was mutual.

Monique was proud of Liz. She had finally taken Monique's advice and found other interests besides chasing men, like the bowling league she and Monique joined last year, and the all-female Jazzercise class she enjoyed that allowed for exercise without being ogled by the men at the fitness center. When Liz did go out it was usually to the local hangout for a few drinks, where she was surrounded by people she'd known all her life, not strangers she found attractive. During those rare times that she attended social events in Greenville she was no longer one of the "closers," who stayed until the lights came on at the end of the evening. Instead she looked forward to spending time with Adrian on her weekends home.

"Okay, bride of mine, what's on your mind?" Mac whispered.

"Oh, I'm just looking at Liz and Paul. Wouldn't it be funny if something really took off between them? I'm sure it wouldn't be the first time two brothers married two cousins. And if Jerome and Adrian get married our families will really be intertwined."

Mac grinned. "You're succumbing to the urge to be

a matchmaker. We've been married exactly one hour, and here you go marrying everybody else off."

"It's only because I want everyone to be as happy as I am."

They shared a quick kiss before they resumed greeting their guests.

Monique, sprawled in a most unladylike position with her legs on either side of an ottoman in the bridal lounge, raised one leg at a time and inspected her off-white stockings for runs. "Connie, did you know Glenn was bringing Sabrina?"

"He didn't mention it until last night. I think he's trying to avoid talking about it so I won't ask him for details, and I respect his privacy. I'm trying to act like she's just another girl he's dating that I don't know. It's different, though, because I *do* know her, but you do what you've gotta do."

"Connie, sometimes I think it's too bad you didn't have more kids. You're a model mother," Monique said. "I wish *my* mom knew when to step back. She drove me nuttier than a pecan pie during the plans for the wedding. She wanted me to get one of those frilly bridal gowns with the poufy sleeves, like I'm twenty years old or something."

Connie laughed.

"And she was all over the menu," Monique continued. "You should have heard her fuss when I told her Mac and I decided to serve Bill's Hot Dogs cut into bite-sized pieces at the cocktail hour."

"They went over big. Everybody loves Bill's."

"Mom thought they were tacky. I think she actually lost sleep over worrying about what people would say, like I give a pluck." Monique shook her head. "And she must have asked me fifty times if Mac and I are going to have kids, starting the moment I told her we were engaged. I'm forty-one, not twenty-five. I don't have a crystal ball I can look into. If it happens, it happens. But Mac and I realize time's not on our side, and if it doesn't happen it's okay with both of us."

"That's all that matters, then," Connie said.

"That's all that should matter. But with all I had to deal with on the road to this day, I was beginning to wish I'd done what you and Lyman did, a quiet ceremony and luncheon for the closest of family and friends."

"It's different for us, Monique. We'd both been married before and gone through all the pomp and circumstance. I think everyone should do it once, but once is enough. As for kids, well, maybe Lyman and I will have one." At Monique's dubious glance she added, "I was only kidding. I'm forty-seven, remember? I might still *look* good"—Connie and Lyman had gone on a joint diet and were both about twenty-five pounds lighter—"but I know I'm just a hop, skip, and a jump away from hot flashes. Our baby will be the B-and-B."

"I'm so happy you and Lyman decided to buy it from Uncle Teddy, now that I'm leaving and he spends so much time in Charlotte."

"We're going to miss you, Monique. Lyman and I will give you and Mac a special rate when you come to visit."

"We're counting on it."

Monique felt Mac squeeze her hand and she leaned toward him. "Look at Jerome and Adrian," he said. "They make a nice couple, don't they?"

Her eyes went to the dancing couple. "Yes, they do. And to think we all said it would never last."

"I think that whatever happens, what they've got is the real thing. I'm glad there was more to it than reckless sex. But they're at a stage when they might still grow apart, being at different colleges and all."

"Maybe if Adrian was in Asheville or someplace clear across the state, but there's really not that much distance between Raleigh and Elizabeth City. Adrian told me they often meet to spend weekends at the halfway point since the semester started."

"I guess time will tell." He kissed her hand. "What about us?"

"We're going to be together forever. Eventually you're going to build us a new house with your own two hands, but in the meantime I'm going to turn the other bedroom of your—I mean *our*—house into a spacious, bright office for me, where I can entertain my muse."

"And write best-selling fiction," he added. Monique hadn't been successful in getting an agent, but she'd been thrilled when a publisher asked to see her full manuscript, only to be devastated when it was returned to her. At first she'd been tempted to put the entire thing through a shredder, but the letter sent with it was encouraging, indicating they would be interested in seeing a revised version. It had taken four more months of frenzied labor, but the hard work paid off. Her first novel would be published early the following year, and her contract—she'd engaged the services of an attorney to interpret it for her while she began a renewed agent search—called for her to write another. Her second manuscript would be even more challenging because she'd put so much energy into plotting the first one that she had no idea what her second would be about. She believed she had what it took to write one book, but writing two and continuing from there was something else.

Liz slipped into her seat on Mac's other side. "Look at my beautiful daughter," she said proudly as she beamed at Adrian.

"She's a beauty, all right," Mac agreed.

"I still can't believe she's in college. But you know what? If she makes a loving marriage that lasts—after she graduates from college, of course—when my time comes I'll die a happy woman."

"You're not going anywhere any time soon, Liz," Mac said. "You've got a lot of good years ahead of you."

"Well, my future is looking pretty bright these days, but I want Adrian to do better than me. I don't want her to be a single mother, even if her ex lives on the next block rather than halfway around the world. It's hard, no matter what the circumstances. Of course, with Jerry stationed in Thailand it's been exceptionally hard for me, but I want Adrian to have a good, solid marriage, the kind I didn't get to have."

Monique leaned across Mac. "Liz, you've only just turned forty-two. There's still plenty of time for you to find that special someone. Look at how long it took for me to get married." But much as Monique hated to hear Liz so pessimistic about her future, she couldn't help thinking her attitude might actually be beneficial. If she would stop hoping to meet that special man around every corner, he'd probably turn up. Maybe he already had, she thought, looking at Paul as he socialized with other guests. "But I'm glad you've softened toward Jerome."

"No point in holding a grudge. Besides, there's

nothing I can really do now to keep them apart. They're adults." She shuddered. "Gosh, it's hard for me to say that about my baby. But I'm determined not to be like Diane and Arthur. I don't feel I have to be included in every facet of Adrian's life. Adrian still needs me, of course, but I won't be afraid to let go completely when the time comes."

"Speaking of which, did you know their daughter is Glenn's date?"

"I saw. Lotsa luck to him is all I can say. I don't think her parents will be satisfied with anyone she chooses, even though Glenn's a good boy from a good home. They're the types to think no one is good enough for their little girl. I hope he knows what he's getting into by dating a girl whose parents are such clinging vines. Personally, I give it six weeks."

"Liz!"

"I'm not kidding. If Glenn and Sabrina get married down the road I can picture Diane and Arthur now, showing up uninvited on their doorstep every other day."

"Uh . . . ladies, I'm beginning to feel like I don't even need to be here, with the two of you chirping away like blackbirds," Mac said good-naturedly, but firmly.

Monique promptly straightened up and sat back in her chair. She'd just stood before God and promised to honor Mac. All right, so she'd promised to honor *Russell*, but the name didn't matter. He'd just indicated that their leaning over him to chitchat annoyed him, and that meant it was time to stop. She and Liz could get together for a real chat next week, after she and Mac returned from their honeymoon in Key West and were settled in Raleigh.

"Are you kidding?" she said to Mac. "This show wouldn't fly without you." She reached for his hand and raised it, rubbing the back of it against her cheek.

"Uh-oh. I think the newlyweds are about to get sickening," Liz said in a teasing manner. She cupped her ear with her hand. "Oops. I think I hear Adrian calling me. Or Paul. Or somebody. *Anybody.* Just get me away from these two." She flashed a grin, and with a swish of tulle she was gone.

Mac looked at his bride carefully, then followed her gaze to where Teddy stood with his date, a widow he'd met in Charlotte on one of his many visits to Reggie's. "Does it bother you to see your uncle with another lady?"

She chuckled. He knew her so well. "No, not really. Even after all this time it's still a little weird to see him with her—Reggie said the same thing—but 'bother' isn't the right word. Reggie's happy for him, and so am I." She sighed. "Not to take anything away from Uncle Teddy, but I just wish it had been as easy for Mrs. Morgan to find someone."

"Is that the lady who caused all the ruckus at the dance last year?"

"That's the one. She's here. Alone, I might add. I see her at the cemetery a lot, tending to her husband's grave. I guess there really are more eligible women than men."

"Maybe she'll meet someone one day," Mac said.

"I don't mean to sound morose," she said apologetically.

"I understand. You'd like Mrs. Morgan to be as happy as Teddy seems to be."

"You know, Peggy would be glad he's not alone. She was that type of person, completely unselfish and very wise. I hope that one day I'll be like her. Or like Connie. You know, she predicted over a year ago that Uncle Teddy had met someone special in Charlotte." She sighed. "But I do so wish Aunt Peggy could have been here."

"I'm sorry I never got to meet her. But I'll always be grateful to her. It was because of her that you came to Washington to stay for a while."

"Yes, when Uncle Teddy was having trouble taking care of her and running the B-and-B at the same time. Funny. Aunt Peggy always wanted me to live in Washington. She said she believed I'd find what I was looking for here. Of course, I thought she was nuts." She chuckled at the memory. "I had a great time here while I was growing up, but when I was grown I saw just how small Washington really is. Yet, when I moved here I met you, and even though we'll be living in Raleigh, here we are, bound to each other for the rest of our lives."

Mac raised a playful eyebrow. "You make it sound like a death sentence."

"If it is, then what a way to go. But it's so strange. It really makes a person wonder if Aunt Peggy somehow could have known I'd find true love here."

At that precise moment the room went dark, startling everyone present. A collective cry filled the air, and a frightened Monique reached for her husband's hand, but the lights flickered back on after just a few seconds, and the party resumed. Monique and Mac stared at each other, then at the ceiling lights, and then back at each other.

He kissed her hand, which he still held. "I think she knew," he said.

Dear Reader,

Things change.

I've certainly learned that over the last year. I'd had high-speed DSL service through DirectTV for a year-and-a-half when I was notified that DirecTV was shutting down its Internet division. The timing couldn't have been worse, as my latest book *Closer Than Close* was just hitting the stores. To anyone who e-mailed me and didn't receive a reply or had their e-mail returned undeliverable, rest assured I was not trying to ignore you. Your comments are what keep me going on those rare occasions when I'm worn out and feel I can't write my name, much less another novel. I can't tell you how sorry I am this happened. I have switched my DSL service to BellSouth, which I think it's safe to say will be around for awhile.

Likewise, I had had the same mailing address ever since my husband and I moved into our house more than four years ago. It was small post office outlet inside a Boxes-n-Bows gift wrap store in the local mall, but last spring the owners announced they were retiring, and I had to get a mailbox at one of the local post offices. At least this time it included mail forwarding for one year.

My new e-mail and mailing addresses appear at the bottom of this page.

That said, I hope you enjoyed reading about one woman's metamorphosis in *Straight to the Heart*. Monique

Oliver originally appeared in my third book, *Love Affair*, as a woman about to lose a man she thought was hers. Her losing streak at love, due to her own over-confidence and self-absorption, was briefly mentioned in subsequent books. And then I began to get these strong feelings about trying to redeem her and give her a happy ending on her own. The result is what you've just read.

As far as what's coming next, some of you have asked me to do a story on either Chantal or Sinclair Hatchet, the much-younger sisters of Cornelia "Hatch" Hatchet in *From This Day Forward*. While I know time tends to move faster than "dog years" in books and on TV, I can't get comfortable making someone who was a mere teenager in 2001, mature into her mid-twenties just three years later. Maybe when a little more time has passed. Instead, I'm considering a request that other readers have made about another character in *From This Day Forward*. Those of you who wanted to know more about that quickie Vegas marriage that broke Lucien Ballard's heart will be happy to know I'm outlining that story now.

As always, wishing you good reading!

Bettye

Bettye Griffin
P.O. Box 54695
Jacksonville, Florida 32245

E-mail: bundie@bellsouth.net

Web site: www.bettyegriffin.com

Bettye Griffin is the author of seven novels. Originally from Yonkers, New York, she currently resides in Jacksonville, Florida, with her husband. She is presently working on her eighth title for Arabesque. Visit her on the Web at www.bettyegriffin.com.